Mystic Lake

Melissa Saari

Whimsical Publications, LLC

Florida

Mystic Lake is a work of fiction. Names, characters, and incidents are the products of the author's imagination and are either fictitious or are used fictitiously. Any resemblance to actual events or persons, living or dead, is entirely coincidental.

To purchase the authorized electronic edition of *Mystic Lake*, visit
www.whimsicalpublications.com

Cover art by Shyanne England
Editing by Brieanna Robertson

ISBN-13: 978-1-63492-028-2

Published by
Whimsical Publications, LLC
Florida

Kelly stepped down hard on the top of the stepladder. It only had three steps, but somehow Virgil had managed to botch the assembly. Two bolts tore loose from the hinges on the stepladder, and Kelly started to fall backward. It all happened so fast that she had no time to react as she plummeted to the floor and landed on her back with no support.

A terrible, tearing pain shot through Kelly's abdomen when she landed. She fought for air and cried out in pain. Panic stirred inside her, and her hands were wrapped around her abdomen to try and ease the pain, so she couldn't get to her feet.

"Are you all right?" asked Virgil.

"I'm in a lot of pain right now. I think the baby might have gotten hurt."

"Kelly! Oh my God, we've got to get you to a hospital. Can you stand up?" Kelly put her elbows against the floor, but it was no use.

While she lay on her back, the fear kept getting worse, and it started to turn into anger. "I thought you said you put that stepladder together correctly."

"I did! I mean, how hard could it be? It only has three steps. Give me your hand."

"I don't know, you were the one that put it together," she answered. She raised her arm, but it almost felt like defeat.

He messed up the stepladder, but now I have to rely on him.

She found the strength to grab Virgil's hand, and he pulled her to her feet. When she stood, she got dizzy at once.

"The room is spinning," said Kelly.

Virgil took a firm grip on her other shoulder. "Kelly, you're bleeding. There's no time to argue, I'm taking you to the hospital."

Kelly let Virgil walk her to the car, because when she saw the red stain spreading on the floor, she got even dizzier.

Virgil took care of Kelly, walking her to the truck so she wouldn't fall a second time. It seemed to take forever to get to the hospital, and when she looked out the window, it made her vertigo come back.

At the hospital, chaos surrounded her as she tried to get checked in. One person at the desk wanted to know how long she had been pregnant, and she was trying to answer, but the nurse was taking her blood pressure and telling her not to talk.

Kelly didn't like the feeling when she sat down on the hospital bed. Her hands were tingling, and her thoughts were racing. The nurse asked her if she was allergic to anything, and she said no. They asked Virgil too, and he agreed.

Once she was in the bed, a nurse made sure she had an IV in her arm. "You need to get liquid inside you because you're dehydrated badly. The doctor will be checking on you in a minute."

She felt a little better, but she had no idea when the doctor would show up. Virgil handed her tissues, as she needed them to dry her eyes, and the expression of caring helped a lot. She was surprised when the male doctor with a nametag she couldn't pronounce arrived a few minutes later, as promised.

Virgil stood up and held her hand when the doctor came in. She didn't object, but his hand was even colder than hers. Worse, he was shaking a little bit, and this added to her insecurity.

"And you are?" asked the doctor, looking at Virgil first.

"I'm the father," he said, taking a bigger puff of air than necessary.

"You're going to wait outside then."

"Why?" he asked, still holding her hand.

"It's the rules," said the doctor.

Virgil let go of her hand. Falling silent, he left the room.

"You're going to need an ultrasound." The doctor had a downcast frown.

"Yeah, I know, and the gel is really cold, isn't it?"

"You've had ultrasounds before. All these hospitals stay nice and cool, and so does the gel, but we still need to see what's going on."

Kelly relented and lifted her shirt. The coldness made her belly flinch. Her exposed skin caught every draft and made it feel like it was snowing on her.

She didn't mind the ultrasound tool swishing back and forth on her belly, because the friction made the gel warmer. The doctor kept scanning back and forth, but his frown only deepened a tiny bit.

"There's no second heartbeat," he said, as if it was just a matter of fact.

"But you can see my baby, right?"

"Yes, he's right here, but his heart has stopped. The umbilicus is loose, so all the signs are there. You've had a miscarriage."

Kelly stared at the doctor, but his face bore the same frown.

"You're saying I lost the baby?"

The doctor nodded once, but Kelly was already starting to grieve by the time he tried to change the subject.

Acknowledgements

This book is dedicated to Lloyd Wilhelm, who always makes me think on my toes.

Also by
Melissa Saari

The Red Satin Shoes
Blue Satin Diary

Curse of the Lion People
Curse of the Black Dragon

The Legend of the Pirate Queen (coming soon)

Chapter One

Kelly sat at home, relaxing on her bed, but her friends were all dressed up and ready to go. She had a shorter dress on, more like a skirt really, but her friends had fancy hairdos, and Tammy even had a small tiara balanced on her puffed-up curls. Since it was the late 70s, puffy was the style of the day, and the girls didn't mind working on their hair.

The girls lined up in front of Kelly's mirror, arranging their lipstick and their mascara, but Kelly didn't worry about things like that. She didn't even bother with lipstick as the other girls preened themselves.

While they worried about their appearances, Kelly daydreamed about a girl walking through a basement with nothing but a flashlight to light her way. Suddenly, her daydream revealed a ghost sitting on the floor, and when it looked up, it didn't have any eyes.

"Aren't you coming with us to the game?" asked Tammy.

Kelly opened her notebook, desperate to write the idea down before it went away.

"No, I'm going to pass. I actually had a good idea for a story."

Kelly had managed to write *ghost with no eyes* in her notebook.

"Nonsense," answered Tammy. "You're coming along with us this time. When was the last time you were on a real date?"

"It wasn't really a date, Tammy. It was Halloween, and he drank some apple cider with me, but I don't even remember his name. Besides, there was a hay ride and I didn't want to get hay on my legs."

Tammy tried to hide her reaction with her hand, but her eyes couldn't hide their sparkles. "But he wanted you to come along. He was probably planning on kissing you when you were on the cart."

"I know, but the hay is always poking my skin. I can't concentrate on a boy if my tush is all itchy." Kelly wanted to keep arguing, but that ghost with no eyes popped into her mind again, with a dress from the twenties or so. She opened her notebook once more and managed to write down *old-fashioned dress* before Tammy talked to her again.

"If you keep writing, you're going to miss the whole game."

Kelly closed her notebook, but the more Tammy pestered her, the more she wanted to bring her notebook to the football game.

"I have to get these ideas down on paper. What if they don't come back?"

"Kelly, when you get to the football game, there won't be anything to distract you. Just look at all the boys and see which one looks nice to you. And please don't keep your nose in that notebook the whole time or you won't be able to spot a good catch."

Stacey couldn't help chucking in agreement, and Kelly shot her an angry glare.

"I wish I had a date for the prom," she said.

"I don't mind dancing alone," Kelly shot back.

"Well, I do," said Tammy. "It's a lot better when you've got someone's fingers wrapped around your lower back. Don't worry, they're usually afraid to grab your butt."

Kelly wished she had enough nerve to say why she didn't want to go. The idea for the story pushed into her mind again, and she could see the little ghostly toes on her feet. She wanted to tell Tammy that she had another new idea, but she knew Tammy would just laugh at her and insist all the more that she come to the game.

She managed to write *no shoes* before Tammy interrupted her again.

"Well, come on then! We need to get there before the game starts, don't we?"

Kelly didn't usually go to football games. In fact, she'd missed the entire season, and this was the last game. She didn't find anything special about the last game, but her classmates took it seriously, and sometimes, it was hard to ignore her friends.

Kelly followed after them, but when the wind caught her knees, she remembered that the Montana winds still blew just as fierce in May as they did in January. She pulled her coat closer and fell back behind her friends a few steps. She didn't wander too far, though. She didn't want to get kidnapped or anything.

Most kidnappings happen close to home. People could be hiding in the bushes, just waiting to jump out.

Kelly heard the noisy crowd at the football game before she could see the bleachers.

I hate loud people in crowds, but at least they won't pay any attention to me. That would make me easier to kidnap.

The story continued to develop in her mind, about a girl that got kidnapped and the police couldn't hear her screams because of the noisy football stadium nearby. She caught up to Tammy so she could complain.

"I just had another great idea, but you wouldn't let me bring my notebook."

Tammy took the complaint in stride, popping out a response faster than Kelly expected. "Well, tell me about it, and I'll remind you later."

"It doesn't work that way, you know that. It's already going away. There it goes."

"I'm sure the idea will come back. Just try really hard to remember it."

Kelly still remembered, but if she admitted that, she wouldn't have any leverage on Tammy. She fell quiet instead, that way Tammy would have no idea what she was thinking.

Although the stadium was never able to charge for football game attendance, they had a sign that begged for a 25-cent donation. Kelly dropped the requested quarter into the bucket, and most of her friends did, but Stacey was so poor that she couldn't even provide the quarter. She dropped two nickels into the metal bucket instead.

Kelly looked at the paltry collection of coins in the metal basin, much smaller than a milk pail, but still too big to hold the tiny pile of coins at the bottom. She estimated about three dollars of change in there.

"I'd be happy to donate more than this!" said Tammy.

"How does ten dollars sound? Would that help the team?"

Tammy pulled a roll of quarters and peeled the brown wrapper away like a pack of Life Savers.

It must be nice when your mom is a bank teller.

The gangly teenager in eyeglasses was too excited to sit down anymore, but even standing up, he couldn't hide how skinny his arms and legs were.

"The Friends of the Bozeman Hawks would gratefully accept this donation."

Kelly was surprised at the condition of the bleachers when she walked up to the stands. A fence protected the underside of the bleachers, but it didn't hide the rust on the struts and the bright neon remains of sodas still clinging to the metal.

When she could see the seats, it looked even worse. No one had bothered to add cushions to the metal seats, and no backrests existed at all.

The catwalk was just wide enough to walk along, and even when she sat down, it felt unsteady. She was able to rock it back and forth with her feet.

After she sat down, she wanted to lean back, but she remembered there was no backrest. She had to lean forward instead, and the metal seats had little ridges in them that started to grind against her hips.

The game hasn't even started yet. My hips are going to be killing me by the time I get out of here.

"Are you comfortable?" asked Tammy in a cheery voice.

"Oh, I'm feeling wonderful," she answered, not caring that it made her dishonest.

Kelly shifted against the seat, still feeling the ridges dig into her thighs, but the wait was almost over. The cheerleaders were doing their noisy routines, and the snare drums announced the players.

She didn't think much of the cheerleaders, especially Danielle, the anorexic leader. Each one sported identical breasts and lips, making it hard to tell them apart, except for Danielle, who was even skinnier than the rest.

At the end of the performance, the girls all created a pyramid, climbing up on top of each other. She wasn't surprised to see Danielle standing atop the pyramid, but her eyes opened wide when she jumped off and stuck the landing.

She bounced away with the rest of the cheerleaders, and she didn't even limp. Kelly knew that if she did that, she would break an ankle at least.

A lot of wolf whistles broke out from the men in the bleachers.

The opposing team ran out first, one at a time, until all the athletes were on the field. Each one of them sported bright gold uniforms, although she knew it wasn't real gold. She couldn't think of a single high school with that kind of money.

"Please welcome the Billings Golden Bears!"

A whole bunch of people started shouting and booing at the Billings football players. The uniforms covered them so well that all she could see were the helmets turning toward the bleachers. Kelly stayed seated.

What is the point of making fun of them anyway? They're still going to win.

The home team ran onto the field, dressed in yellow football uniforms. The pads made it almost impossible to see the players. All that stuck out were their arms and legs.

I wasn't missing anything.

"Please welcome the Bozeman Hawks!" The announcer sounded excited, but it didn't seem exciting to Kelly. "Please remove your hats for the National Anthem."

All the football players kneeled and waited as the special guest walked forward to perform the song. Kelly noticed that one of the players on the home team was watching her instead of the singer.

At first glance, she thought he was looking in her direction, but she wasn't sure. She thought he might be looking at one of her friends, but none of them seemed to react to him, or even notice that he wasn't paying attention.

The longer he watched her from the field, the more curious she got about him. She memorized the number on his uniform—28—because she couldn't make out his face very well and his body was covered up with padding.

While her friends got starry-eyed about the young man singing the National Anthem, Kelly focused on the football player. Stacey was trying to blink away tears as the song reached its finale.

The crowd roared in appreciation, and anything her

friends might have said was drowned out by the wall of sound. Once the screaming ended, the game began.

Kelly tried to enjoy it, but when everyone else stood up for the wave, she would stay seated. She kept waiting for someone to fall out of the bleachers when they stood up too fast, but she wasn't going to be that person.

As the game progressed, she noticed that 28 was not quite on his best game. One time he missed a pass, which went bouncing off the field instead, and later, he actually dropped the football.

She wasn't sure what was throwing him off, but it made the game more entertaining to her. She was surprised when he carried the ball all the way to the touchdown, because she'd expected someone else to take the pass, since 28 was doing so bad. When he also got the kick between the bars, winning the game, she was even more surprised.

Even though everyone else cheered loudly throughout the game, Kelly kept quiet. She didn't want to ruin her voice.

After the game ended, everyone went home, and Kelly was able to go back to her room by herself. No one was bothering her anymore, and she could focus on the story.

Chapter Two

Kelly ran into the football player the following Monday when she was getting her books from her locker. She hadn't been able to see his body under the uniform, but every muscle in his arms was sculpted and bulged whenever he flexed.

"I saw you at the game yesterday," he said by way of introduction. "I've never seen you there before."

She hesitated, but then decided to tell the truth. "I've never been to a game before. I usually spend my time writing."

Now it was the football player's turn to pause. She hoped that she hadn't said the wrong thing. A football came spinning through the air over her shoulder and he grabbed it before it could hit anyone.

She noticed that his arm moved fast enough for her to not see it rising, and she realized how skilled he actually was.

"Hey, Virgil, now I know why you missed that pass!" yelled one of the other football players as they walked past.

"Think fast, Brad!" he shouted back, and the football went spinning back to his teammate. His friend caught the pass and let it bounce on the floor.

"Touchdown!" he shouted. His friend piped up, happy to join the mockery.

Wow, he really is good at football.

"Virgil's got a girlfriend!"

"Get out of here, Jack!" shouted Virgil, and the two players headed off down the hallway.

Kelly was grateful for the good luck, because now she didn't have to ask what his name was. She could use that time for better questions.

Virgil started to look embarrassed. "I never even caught your name," he said after a couple seconds.

"I'm Kelly," she answered.

"Kelly, can I take you out to dinner sometime?"

He asked me a question first. He really likes me.

Kelly had never been asked on a date before. It took her by surprise, and she didn't know what to say at first. She assumed that he had caved to peer pressure, but he kept watching her with raised eyebrows, sincere almost to the point of desperation. In that moment of hesitation, she jumped at the first excuse that came to mind.

"I don't know, restaurants cost money. I don't think I can afford it."

Virgil laughed out loud. "Don't worry, I'll cover it."

Okay, so he doesn't even mind that I don't have any money.

"All right, it's a date."

Virgil smiled from ear to ear. "Now Brad and Jack can't pick on me anymore."

Kelly smiled too, though inside she was wondering what to do when she was on the date.

She decided to talk with Tammy at the lunch tables, where she had a little more privacy. It was pizza day and the pizza appeared less gross than usual. She was able to find an area with less people around to overhear them talking.

They wouldn't believe a girl like me could get a date.

Tammy fussed with a napkin in her lap before she started to eat the pizza.

"Virgil asked me out on a date."

Tammy got excited enough to put down her pizza. "That's wonderful. You don't seem so withdrawn anymore."

Kelly tried to wipe the sweat off her hands, and she recognized the excitement she felt before she could dry her hands completely. "I've never been to a nice dinner," she said. "What do I wear?"

"I've got just the thing," answered Tammy. "You leave that to me. Do you know how to fold a napkin?"

"Not really, no. I saw one in a wedding a long time ago."

Tammy lifted her napkin and spread it out on the table. She deftly made four points, pulled them to the middle, and did a twist to bring the points together. It ballooned into a kite and settled neatly on the table.

Kelly tried to memorize it, but it was impossible. "What goes on with that twist?" she asked.

Tammy laughed. "You don't have to do it just like that," she said. "Here, let me show you again."

Once Kelly learned to fold her napkin, Tammy showed her the finer points of drinking without losing eye contact, and how the spoon, fork, and knife all had their place, but that was something she was more used to. By the end of the lunch, she felt like she had a much better idea of what she was doing.

Later that afternoon, Tammy showed up at her house. This time, Kelly was the one getting lipstick and rouge and mascara. Tammy even fixed her hair up in curlers, so it would be nice and fluffy. She was amazed at the difference.

Kelly thought she already looked stunning, but Tammy presented her with a purple evening gown. She didn't have any dresses that fancy, so she was almost afraid she would tear it. Tammy kept encouraging her, and once the straps were in place, she felt like a woman instead of her actual age, a woman old enough to have a drink.

When Tammy walked her downstairs, her parents' eyes opened wide. When they noticed how well Tammy had done her makeup, they looked at her with a new kind of respect. Both of her parents were taller than she was, but she felt like they were looking up to her.

At the restaurant, Virgil showed her even more respect and politeness than she'd ever expected. Not only did he escort her, he pulled the chair out for her and everything. Once he sat down, he started to arrange his napkin at once. Kelly arranged her napkin too, but she had been practicing and got it done a little faster than Virgil.

He looked up in surprise when she lowered the perfect napkin to her lap while he was still folding his own. A broad smile crossed his face.

"So, why do you like me so much, Virgil?" she asked. She expected him to think for a while, but his answer was immediate.

"You're not like the other people that I know, Kelly. You don't have a mean bone in your body. Even the other football players are complete brutes."

"That's what I really like about you," said Kelly. "The way you can catch the football so fast, and run down the field, but you're not actually trying to hurt the other players."

"I've never been good at tackling, but you have to under-stand that's the front line's job."

Kelly didn't think that much of sports, but when Virgil talked about it, the idea of two different lines of players made sense, and she felt like trying out other new experi-ences, learning more ideas. She was so caught up in his con-versation that the next comment broke down all her bounda-ries.

"You're such a nice person, Kelly. No one knows how to fold napkins anymore. Some girls try to be sweet, but you're actually sincere about it."

She tried to keep some self-awareness, but the tugging from her heart was too strong, and she found herself think-ing about Virgil instead of worrying about anything else.

They were both too young to drink anything intoxicating, but even the soda was served in tall glasses. She noticed that he was careful not to lose eye contact while he sipped his drink, and she did the same. It was so refreshing to her that she could encounter a person that was polite for a change.

It was something she hadn't known she could wish for, because the rudeness of the other boys at school was intol-erable, between them burping and leaving their trash at the table and writing jokes on the side of walls. With Virgil, she could see a future where she wouldn't have to put up with that type of rude behavior anymore, and she doubted that it could be anything but a blessing.

When they were done eating, she realized that she was falling in love with Virgil.

Chapter Three

Kelly sat down in the cafeteria on Monday and everything was different. Tammy was grinning, and the other girls were smirking too.

"You've got one hot boyfriend now, Kelly," said Sarah. "I don't know how you got so lucky!"

Kelly grinned, enjoying being the center of attention for a change. "He's such a polite kind of guy."

"That's why you can't get close to someone like that," said Brenda. "You have no idea how to be polite."

"Oh, and you do?" Sarah shot back. She drank from her milkshake with a lot of noise.

Tammy had to cough to get Sarah's attention, but Sarah shut her mouth once she noticed Tammy's disapproving glare. "You don't have to be that noisy just to prove your point, Sarah. That's pretty rude." Tammy gave her a serious look.

"You don't know him at all," said Kelly. "He might play football, but he's a gentle giant. He pulled the chair out for me. He opened the car door, the restaurant door. It was amazing."

"You don't have to rub it in our faces now," said Sarah, shooting her a wink, so she knew at once it was in fair play.

"Well, why didn't we think of that before?" asked Brenda. "We just have to be nice and then we'll get studs too."

"Well, I never accused you of being smart," said Tammy.

***

Kelly woke up a few days later and was sick to her stomach at once. She didn't have a lot of time to get to the toilet and she stumbled because she was so sleepy.

The smell of coffee wafted up from downstairs, and it bothered her stomach.

The smell of coffee has never bothered me before.

The second time it happened, she knew for sure that something was going on, and she had a pretty good idea what that was. Just to be sure, she stopped by the health clinic on the way to school. She didn't mention that she wasn't 18 yet, and they forgot to ask, which helped out a lot. When they ran the tests, though, she was surprised at how fast it came back positive.

The doctor raised his eyebrows at once. "You're pregnant, young lady."

Kelly was beside herself with shock. "I am?"

"At least two months along, from what I can tell. It was the morning sickness, wasn't it?"

"How did you know about that?" she asked.

"It's the first sign," he said.

"The smell of coffee made it happen," she said.

"Well, I know this is going to be tough, but you're going to have to stay away from coffee. When you're carrying a baby, you need all the nutrition you can get. Try some milkshakes instead. Now you'll be feeding two people."

Kelly tried to fathom this new situation. It wasn't something she'd expected from her first sexual encounter.

"What else do I need to know?" she asked. "Isn't this going to be a lot of work? Should I sit differently? Can I still drink soda without popping?"

The doctor looked like he was getting tired of her questions, but he leaned back and took it all in stride. "Let's just answer these things one at a time. You're going to feel tired, but that's just because of your growing baby. You'll get angry too fast, but that's to be expected with the burden you're carrying. Second, your body knows what to do. There's no exercise you need to worry about or anything. You're supposed to add weight when you're carrying a baby, and don't let anyone tell you otherwise."

Kelly tried to listen carefully, but she wished she had brought a notepad.

"Take it easy, drink plenty of water, whatever you feel like eating, and I'm sure you have some hobbies, don't you?"

"Oh, yes, I write as often as I can," answered Kelly. New

opportunities for using her craft were suddenly appearing, and true happiness flowed through her.

"You don't have to sit any different than you are. You're not going to hurt the baby by leaning forward or whatever. It's surrounded by water and protected by your body. Come back and see me in a month, and a month after that, when we get closer to your due date, we can make appointments more often."

Kelly tried to keep all this knowledge in her mind. None of the advice was surprising to her, but she did notice how hungry she was. She thought that a good meal would make her feel better.

When the school day ended, Virgil walked home with her. She wasn't used to this kind of attention and she was happy about it, but people sitting on their front porches rocked back and forth and could hear what she said, so she couldn't tell Virgil about the baby.

The weight of the knowledge was a lot for her to bear, and she noticed that her hands were across her belly, trying to protect it from harm. She wanted to keep her hands there once she noticed, but she realized that other people would notice, and she didn't want to reveal anything too soon.

She opened the front door, hoping to get to her bedroom, but her parents piped up when she got inside.

"Hello, Kelly. Good afternoon, Virgil."

Kelly didn't want to say anything, so she kept walking toward the stairs. Virgil stopped and waved, though, so she stopped and tried not to glare at him while he socialized.

"Hello to both of you," answered Virgil. "You changed your hair color, didn't you, ma'am?"

"I'm so glad you noticed," answered Kelly's mother.

Kelly glared at Virgil, and he finally started moving toward the staircase. She didn't stop moving until she got to her bedroom. Virgil got there a few seconds later.

"What's going on, Kelly?"

Kelly turned around, astonished that her bedroom door was still open. She rushed over to close it at once. "Do you want my parents to hear me?"

"I don't see why not," answered Virgil.

Kelly took a deep breath, but she was almost ready to change her mind about telling him. "Virgil, I don't want you to start shouting or anything, but I'm pregnant."

Virgil looked stunned. He opened his mouth wide. Kelly thought for sure he was about to yell, and she braced for his reaction. She was relieved when he caught himself and spoke in a hushed voice.

"You're going to have my baby?"

Kelly nodded.

"That's incredible news. Why don't you want your parents to know?"

"Isn't it obvious? What would they say? I'm not eighteen yet for another three months."

Virgil pressed his fingers against his closed eyes and slowly squeezed the bridge of his nose. "I'm still going to have to tell my parents, though."

Kelly started to panic. She felt like her chest was going to cave in. Pain shot through her ribs on both sides of her lungs and she thought she might even be starting to have a heart attack. She started breathing way too fast, and only her focus on slowing down her breathing saved her from fainting. She saw spots in her vision and her hands felt tingly, but she was able to gasp out, "Oh, please don't do that."

Virgil grabbed her hands, and she held on for dear life. He might not have been expecting the reaction, but he was more than capable of keeping her hands in a firm, comforting grip. "Kelly, this is serious. I can't just run away from this, and even if I did, my parents would still hunt me down. I'm going to tell them what's going on, and hopefully, they aren't going to be too upset."

She knew her emotions were getting back under control, and the shakiness was gone from her words. "And what about my parents?"

"I don't know, Kelly, but it's not like this was an accident."

Kelly shook her head. "No, it wasn't an accident, but my parents are still going to be mad at me anyway."

"Why would they be mad? My parents are always telling me that having babies is what makes women so special."

Kelly couldn't help but accept the fact that this was going to be a good thing, but the idea of raising a child at home, with her parents watching her change the diapers, was scary indeed. "My mother has mentioned that to me a few times, about how important it is to have babies, but not when I'm living at home."

Virgil leaned back, scratching his head. "I don't have unlimited resources, but it would make sense to get ourselves a little place of our own."

Kelly stayed on the bed while Virgil got up, paced, and finally walked away. Kelly leaned back with caution, using her elbows to lower herself to the bed. Once she could feel the blanket beneath her, she was sure she wouldn't hurt the baby, and she started to relax.

Deep inside, something stirred, and Kelly wondered how she would be able to tell the difference between her gut instincts, which were quite strong sometimes, and the baby moving inside her.

Chapter Four

The next time Virgil came over, he was smiling from ear to ear. Kelly saw his grin as he walked up to the house. Stomach cramps had started in the morning, and it sometimes made her feel unsteady, so she hadn't been downstairs except for breakfast.

Virgil sat down on the bed next to her. "I found a place for us to live. It's not in very good shape, but there's enough room for you and me and the baby. I only had to spend five hundred dollars, and we actually own it. We'll never have to pay rent."

Kelly grabbed his hand at once. "That's wonderful, Virgil. Thank you so much." At the moment, she truly meant what she said. The gift of a new place to live was not something she could take lightly, but the cramps from her belly felt like warnings sometimes instead of cramps. Virgil kept his hand folded against hers, and the warm comfort of his steady grip made her feel protected and understood.

Kelly started massaging her belly. It seemed to help the cramping, and she wanted it to stop so she could help move her things. "What about all the packing? I can't be carrying heavy boxes around."

"Leave that to me," said Virgil. "I'm supposed to be helping you, remember?"

The idea of help was good, but it hadn't been her suggestion.

"Who told you that?"

"My mother."

Kelly stopped rubbing her stomach. "She knows?"

Virgil nodded. "My father does too." He pulled a nickel from his pocket and ran it back and forth across his knuckles.

"And they're not mad at you?"

Virgil kept nudging the coin from knuckle to knuckle, and as it rolled, the sides of the coin became blurred, so she couldn't see where it touched his hand.

Now, was that my gut instinct or just a kick?

"My father said that you're going to be my top responsibility from now on, and I've got to do right by you. My mother said that she found this house because of someone in her church, and she also said that a baby is always a blessing, and a new home for a new baby is a double blessing." Virgil dropped the nickel into his cupped palm and slid it back into his pocket. Kelly felt a very firm kick from the baby.

Now that was a kick.

Kelly stopped massaging her belly. Instead, she placed both hands against the side, where she felt the kick. Deep inside, she could feel a tiny foot poking like a mole deep inside her belly. The rawness of the experience shocked her into a fresh awareness that she was carrying a baby. This was exactly where the baby was, that's exactly how big the foot was, that's what it felt like to get kicked inside.

The self-awareness made her realize that she was going to be a mother. Nurturing the baby would be her highest priority. Defending the baby would also be very high on her list, and she started to feel a cold paranoia welling up inside her, the first flutters of a protective instinct that she'd never noticed in her mind before.

Kelly took another deep breath, letting the emotions ride on, and noticed that Virgil was still sitting by her side. He didn't feel put out by her silence, and she held onto his hand, which he still had not tried to pull away. Now that she had someone's hand to hold, it seemed much more enjoyable than she thought possible.

Chapter Five

On the way over to the new house, Kelly tried to be positive, and the surrounding hills provided some scenery, even though neighbors lived in houses on both sides. The wilderness gave her room for walks without running into neighbors, and the neighbors provided a sense of security if they noticed something amiss.

The next-door neighbor's house had bright blue paint, and it contrasted with the lack of paint on her new house.

Kelly thought the outside of the house left something to be desired. The paint had been added to the walls ages ago, and the rain running down the boards had washed it all away. The remaining paint left the exterior a messy brown with white splotches where the paint had stayed behind.

The house gave her a bad first impression, but it didn't take long before the thrill of living in her own place drove away her bad feelings.

Virgil brought all the boxes in, but she didn't step into the house right away. She wandered around the front yard, trying to make sense of it all as he unloaded box after box. She also wanted to stay out of his way while the boxes were being moved.

The grass had once been green, but no one had been watering it when the house was empty. She found a sprinkler, but the hose attached to it had cracked open in the sunlight.

Two or three lilac bushes, all overgrown, provided a little privacy, but the leaves were so thick she couldn't tell how many bushes were on each side. They wove amongst each other, concealing the thicker trunks behind bright purple sprigs of flowers. She was delighted to see that the plants were bright green and had no shortage of water. It gave her hope that the house would bring a bright future. She couldn't find a hose anywhere in the front yard, but she hoped that one was still in the back.

The house had one door for the entrance, and a back door that she'd seen Virgil open twice already. She was glad he'd learned how to close the door behind himself, because she'd met grown men that left the door wide open, but the politeness Virgil showed her was one of the things that she found attractive.

While he carried the boxes, she looked around the front yard, walking one step at a time to make sure everything was safe for her and the baby. She found some old railroad spikes, but she was able to toss them into a small pile by the huckleberry bushes. She also found a strip of barbed wire, but it was short and easy enough to dispose of. Farther back and up the hill, she found a hose that was still in good condition wrapped around a tree trunk. It took some time to unwrap, but pulling it downhill was much easier than across the level ground between her and the house.

Walking through the house for the first time, her focus was first on the floor. She didn't hear any loose floorboards, but there were a few places where the floor bowed in between the beams.

The layout was simple enough, and she memorized it quickly. A living room sat next to the kitchen, with a bathroom in the back section, along with a laundry room and a bedroom. A bed already sat in the bedroom, but the blankets were still in the box and the pillows in another box. She was all right with the size of the room, but it just didn't look like a bedroom with everything tucked away in boxes still.

The baby stirred a lot while she walked around. It seemed troubled, like it could sense the new environment. She felt like the baby was excited about the new home as well.

Leaning over, she pulled the sheets from the box, and set about making the bed. It was light work until she got to the blanket. The baby gave her a couple kicks, and she didn't spend a lot of time straightening out the top blanket, keeping her strength up by taking it slow and tugging on one corner at a time.

One of the things she looked for was mold, remembering how dangerous it was for babies. While she scanned the ceilings and walls, she noticed that not one speck of mold was growing on the walls. No water stains muddied the white ceiling tiles. It seemed to be a perfect place to raise a baby.

Kelly left the house and found Virgil by the car, taking a break from unloading boxes. He was squatting by the pile of railroad spikes, counting them as he arranged them in a neater collection.

"It's a nice place," said Kelly, "but could you please buy a new a phone? There is a phone in there somewhere, right?" The idea of not having a phone was distressing to her.

"Well, I didn't see one when I was moving stuff in, but I can ask the landlord about it. Come to think of it, I didn't even notice a phone jack."

"Wouldn't that be the phone company you need to talk to?"

The more answers she got, the worse her heartburn became, and she pushed it off as the pregnancy, because he was trying to help her. She knew that was part of being pregnant, but she was still getting used to asking for things. When she went inside, the heartburn went away, replaced by the joy of having a place of her own. It lifted her spirits to envision growing old and watching her child grow up in the house.

Chapter Six

Kelly was starting to get excited about the new house. She liked sitting in her rocking chair from home and watching her belly get bigger as the baby needed more space to move around.

Virgil sat in an easy chair beside her. With the major repairs done, the minor ones didn't seem so important, and she decided not to bother him about the small things.

Kelly stared at the lonely walls, covered only in floral wallpaper. It was like they were begging for pictures to hide it.

"These walls need some pictures," she said.

"I don't mind them the way they are," answered Virgil. "Those flowers are lovely."

"I have some purple wallpaper I'd like to buy someday."

"We have pictures, though."

Kelly walked over to the box and sat down cross-legged in front of it. Her belly got in the way when she leaned forward, but she was able to open the flaps and start setting the pictures on the carpet.

Looking at the scattered pictures, she noticed the large paintings Virgil had brought—a landscape with no people whatsoever, a very revealing portrait of Marilyn Monroe, and a large photograph of a souped-up Chevrolet truck. She also pulled out a very inspirational picture from her own collection, a whimsical one of fairies among the lily pads. She also added a sampler, one with charming recreations of letters of the alphabet. A house had big bar stitches on the windows, and long, straight stitches for the door. It was a charming collection of different stitches and looked good no matter where it would be resting.

"I'm just going to hang two of them up for now," she said. She set the fairy picture aside and started looking through Virgil's pictures.

"I want the Marilyn," he said.

"Sure," said Kelly, "but I was actually thinking about the landscape picture. It's so breathtaking. I can imagine having a house by a lake someday."

"That's a painting my uncle in Minnesota made, but then an icicle hit him in the wrist and he had to stop painting, so it's really kind of depressing."

"But that's wonderful, Virgil, because you might become a painter too. Isn't it inspiring?" She didn't want to rock the boat too much, but she didn't want the Chevy truck hanging on her wall for years.

"Well, aren't there other pictures in the box?"

"Yes, but they're all from my house."

"Okay, then I'll go with the truck," he answered, and somehow, that seemed like the worst choice to Kelly.

She put the needlework sampler and the truck side by side, and then reversed the positions, which made them look much better.

"Someday, I'll have a truck that's fancier than that one."

"What do they call that thing that goes over the back of the truck there?"

"It's called a canopy," Virgil answered without hesitation.

"I'm glad you know so much about trucks."

"So am I," answered Virgil with a big smile. She wondered how he could have missed the sarcasm in her voice, and then it didn't surprise her so much.

She got back to her feet and went looking for the hammer. Once she found the tool in the laundry room, she went looking for the nails.

Kelly got onto the stepladder so she could get higher up on the wall. She wanted the nails to sit high enough that they wouldn't poke anyone. When she got to the top of the stepladder, it started to wobble. "Virgil, are you sure this thing is stable?"

"Absolutely, I built it myself."

Kelly stepped down and moved it to the side. The wobble left and she felt much steadier.

"We must have a loose beam over there."

"Isn't that a big deal?"

"I'll get around to it," he answered.

She had no trouble getting the first nail through the wall, leaving just enough sticking out to create a hook. Once she got to the second one, though, she had to move the nail back and forth until she knew for sure that she had enough room between the two pictures.

Confident in her decision, she hammered the second nail into place, descended the ladder, and scooted it back over to where the first nail hung. She could feel the strain in her belly, but she paced herself. For a few moments, she had to sit down in the chair, but she made it back to her feet.

When she had her strength back, she made her way back over to the paintings.

Kelly noticed the older string already tied to hooks in the back of the frame. A couple tugs tore the old threads apart, but she had brought plenty of string because it came in handy in a new house. She tugged the string to make sure it was steady, and then got to her feet.

With the nails already in the wall, it was easy for her to lift the picture high enough to slip over the nail. She had to slide the picture back and forth along the string to get it to sit right in the middle, though, and the process took longer than she expected.

As she tried to relax, she could feel the baby kick once, and she decided to stay in the chair. It would give the baby time to calm down, and she would have time to recover too. The baby didn't know what it was doing, but the kick left her intestines sore for a couple minutes.

After she attached the string to the fairy and the truck pictures, she felt much less sore, and the baby had stopped kicking, which was just fine with her.

She got both strings over the nails, but then she stepped down from the chair and gave it a better look and the paintings looked far too close together. She stepped back up onto the chair and got the fairy back down. Then she used the back of the hammer to pull the nail out of the wall. The nail did not want to budge at first. She pulled harder, and then she started to put her weight into it. The nail ripped free all of a sudden.

Kelly stepped down hard on the top of the stepladder. It only had three steps, but somehow Virgil had managed to botch the assembly. Two bolts tore loose from the hinges on the stepladder, and Kelly started to fall backward. It all happened so fast that she had no time to react as she plummeted to the floor and landed on her back with no support.

A terrible, tearing pain shot through Kelly's abdomen when she landed. She fought for air and cried out in pain. Panic stirred inside her, and her hands were wrapped around her abdomen to try and ease the pain, so she couldn't get to her feet.

"Are you all right?" asked Virgil.

"I'm in a lot of pain right now. I think the baby might have gotten hurt."

"Kelly! Oh my God, we've got to get you to a hospital. Can you stand up?" Kelly put her elbows against the floor, but it was no use.

While she lay on her back, the fear kept getting worse, and it started to turn into anger. "I thought you said you put that stepladder together correctly."

"I did! I mean, how hard could it be? It only has three steps. Give me your hand."

"I don't know, you were the one that put it together," she answered. She raised her arm, but it almost felt like defeat.

He messed up the stepladder, but now I have to rely on him.

She found the strength to grab Virgil's hand, and he pulled her to her feet. When she stood, she got dizzy at once.

"The room is spinning," said Kelly.

Virgil took a firm grip on her other shoulder. "Kelly, you're bleeding. There's no time to argue, I'm taking you to the hospital."

Kelly let Virgil walk her to the car, because when she saw the red stain spreading on the floor, she got even dizzier.

Virgil took care of Kelly, walking her to the truck so she wouldn't fall a second time. It seemed to take forever to get to the hospital, and when she looked out the window, it made her vertigo come back.

At the hospital, chaos surrounded her as she tried to get checked in. One person at the desk wanted to know how long she had been pregnant, and she was trying to answer, but the nurse was taking her blood pressure and telling her not to talk.

Kelly didn't like the feeling when she sat down on the hospital bed. Her hands were tingling, and her thoughts were racing. The nurse asked her if she was allergic to anything, and she said no. They asked Virgil too, and he agreed.

Once she was in the bed, a nurse made sure she had an IV in her arm. "You need to get liquid inside you because you're dehydrated badly. The doctor will be checking on you in a minute."

She felt a little better, but she had no idea when the doctor would show up. Virgil handed her tissues, as she needed them to dry her eyes, and the expression of caring helped a lot. She was surprised when the male doctor with a nametag she couldn't pronounce arrived a few minutes later, as promised.

Virgil stood up and held her hand when the doctor came in. She didn't object, but his hand was even colder than hers. Worse, he was shaking a little bit, and this added to her insecurity.

"And you are?" asked the doctor, looking at Virgil first.

"I'm the father," he said, taking a bigger puff of air than necessary.

"You're going to wait outside then."

"Why?" he asked, still holding her hand.

"It's the rules," said the doctor.

Virgil let go of her hand. Falling silent, he left the room.

"You're going to need an ultrasound." The doctor had a downcast frown.

"Yeah, I know, and the gel is really cold, isn't it?"

"You've had ultrasounds before. All these hospitals

stay nice and cool, and so does the gel, but we still need to see what's going on."

Kelly relented and lifted her shirt. The coldness made her belly flinch. Her exposed skin caught every draft and made it feel like it was snowing on her.

She didn't mind the ultrasound tool swishing back and forth on her belly, because the friction made the gel warmer. The doctor kept scanning back and forth, but his frown only deepened a tiny bit.

"There's no second heartbeat," he said, as if it was just a matter of fact.

"But you can see my baby, right?"

"Yes, he's right here, but his heart has stopped. The umbilicus is loose, so all the signs are there. You've had a miscarriage."

Kelly stared at the doctor, but his face bore the same frown.

"You're saying I lost the baby?"

The doctor nodded once, but Kelly was already starting to grieve by the time he tried to change the subject. When the truth hit her, she felt like she was sinking. The feeling was so intense she grabbed the sides of the table to make sure it wouldn't get away from her.

Kelly's hands started to shake, and she tried to control it, but when she couldn't, tears started to flow. Once they started, she couldn't make them stop.

The doctor handed a tissue over to her, but she wasn't sure how long it was offered before she opened her eyes. She accepted the tissue and tried to wipe the tears away.

"The ultrasound also tells me that your left ovary is swollen. There are a number of reasons this could happen, but they all mean that it's going to be difficult for you to have children in the future. It could be a cyst, or maybe five or six, maybe even an infection or a trapped egg."

This second revelation was more heartbreaking than the first. Even with her shirt pulled back down, she still felt cold. To see the future torn away from her so fast was like having a sheet pulled away in the middle of the night.

"I might not get pregnant, and you're saying that could be permanent. Don't you have any good news at all?"

The doctor's frown didn't go away, but his eyes gathered crow's feet at the edges, and she wondered if he was just incapable of smiling.

"The good news is that you came in right away. You could have come down with sepsis or even gangrene. We can take care of you here until you've recovered, so you'll be here for a couple days. We also need to clean you up inside. It won't take long, just a simple curettage, but I'm really glad you showed up."

"But there's nothing you can do for my baby at all?"

"No, I'm sorry, that's beyond our medical expertise. We can't bring him back to life. I'm sorry."

This tragedy was hard for her to fathom, but except for the doctor's apologies, he seemed utterly unbothered by the whole affair. He was very professional, but what Kelly needed was sympathy.

"Can Virgil come back now?"

"Certainly," answered the doctor, stepping out of the room for a moment. She caught a deep sigh of relief from the doctor as he left the room, and she was surprised that he needed to let off steam when she was the one that just lost her baby.

Virgil entered the room and went to her side at once. She had started to calm down, but she was still wiping tears away. The doctor came back into the room too and continued to write notes on his pad.

"I lost the baby," she said, and even though he held her hand, she started to cry again. She wanted to move past the pain and escape it somehow, but the news was so fresh she couldn't really process it.

Virgil kept a tight grip on her hand, and she squeezed his a couple times before she remembered what the doctor said.

"I have to stay here for a couple days. They're going to do a surgery, so can you make sure that you can come back and get me when it's time for me to come back?"

"Oh, of course," he answered. "Anything else?"

"One of my shawls would be nice. It's so cold in these

hospitals."

"All right, I know where one of them is. You want it right now?"

"Of course, Virgil," she answered. "I just feel so cold right now."

The doctor finished with his notes and cleared his throat. "Look, I know this isn't the best time, but there are a few more things I need to mention."

"How can it get worse?" asked Virgil.

"You're going to want to support her for the next few days," said the doctor. "We can't do anything to speed up the process, but her labor is going to start in a couple days. As it gets stronger, the baby will be born, but it's already passed away."

Kelly felt disgust at the news. The contractions had already started, but the next contraction brought a steady increase in pain and the feeling of the dead baby moving inside her made her almost get sick to her stomach.

"So, hold her hand and stuff?" Virgil asked.

"Just be there for her," he answered. "She's going to need you."

Once the doctor left the room, Virgil stayed by her side, holding her hand, and didn't complain when she squeezed as the third contraction hit.

"It's already starting," she said.

"You're going into labor?" he asked.

"Of course, that's what I'm talking about."

Virgil never let go of her hand, but he continued to look upset as she tried to keep breathing through the contraction like she'd been taught.

"Can you tell the doctor that I'm starting my labor pains?" she asked.

"All right then. I'll let him know. I don't think I'll be around when the dead thing comes out, though. Wow, this baby stuff is really gross. I don't know how you women handle this stuff."

Kelly had never expected him to be so rude, especially not at this point in time. The way he just expressed his feelings without any concern for her own made her feel even more disgusting. If he was too big of a coward to stay beside her as the baby left her body, what else was he going to be afraid of? Would he abandon her again? Doubt filled her mind as Virgil walked away.

Virgil left the room, and the click of the door sounded ominous to her.

She could hear Virgil's words through the door. He didn't even lower his voice.

"That dead baby is crawling out of her. I'll be back when it doesn't feel like some horror movie anymore." What he told the doctor must have been just as bad, because she knew the grim look on the doctor's face well enough to recognize an embarrassed man trying to cover up the insults her husband had just spit out. He continued to hold his silence as he walked over to her and checked her heartbeat with his stethoscope. Once he was done, he leaned back and finally spoke to her.

"I'm sorry you have such a cold-hearted man," he said. "You deserve better than that."

She tried to focus on something else, but the steadily increasing cramps in her belly were a prevailing reminder of what had happened. When the baby arrived, she didn't have the energy to lift her head. A nurse walked away, carrying something in her hands, and after that, she was alone.

Chapter Seven

Kelly was sure that Virgil would come back with her shawl pretty soon. Three hours later, though, she had started to wonder. The nurses came and went, and even the apologetic doctor, but still there was no Virgil.

When the doctor showed up again, he was ready, but Kelly was far from it. The long hours without Virgil had made her realize how much she missed him.

The pain was almost unbearable until the numbing injection started to work. The feeling of the needle going into her body was magnified by the cold air, making her skin extra sensitive.

The surgery made her feel dirty, not clean as the doctor insisted. When the doctor was done, he explained that the infection in her ovary had cleared up, but it had probably ruined her remaining eggs.

The next day, she was feeling much better, but Virgil hadn't shown up yet. She called him on the hospital phone after being promised it was free.

"What do you want?" he asked when he picked up.

"I'm all done, and they're ready to let me go home," she said.

"No one called me about it. I thought they were going to call me when you were ready. So is it done?"

"If you mean all the gross things, yes, it's done. They already poked and prodded and everything. I'm supposed to be resting at home now."

After a pause, Virgil asked, "So, why didn't they call me? Did you write the phone number down wrong or something?"

"I gave them the phone number," she answered.

"Well, they didn't write it down correctly, because this is the first time I heard of it. You'll be coming out those glass doors, right?"

"Yes, and you can pull right up front. You found that shawl, right?"

"Oh, yeah, I found that when I got back home."

Kelly paused to wonder and finally got the courage to ask, "Then why didn't you bring it over to me?"

"Well, I didn't know you wanted it right then. Do you want me to come down there or do you want to keep asking me more questions?"

Kelly paused again; she was afraid she would insult him if she continued. "I guess you'd better hang up then."

Unable to wear her ruined dress, she had to leave the hospital in a gown. The shawl was an immediate comfort when she got into the car, but she was still shivering from the air outside.

"Let's get home," said Virgil.

"Are you sure the heater's working in here?" she asked.

"You're practically naked, no wonder you're freezing. Here!"

Virgil stopped the truck for a moment while the heater started to increase the temperature. He pulled off his jacket and handed it to her. She didn't feel particularly impressed, but it was better than nothing. The sleeves were way too long for her arms and stuck out past her hands. It made her freezing hands feel warmer, though, so she decided not to mention it.

When she got home, she wanted to take a hot bath. She turned on the tap full blast and then lowered the tempera-ture until the steam dissipated. She noticed that the water was a little murky, but she ignored it because she wanted to get in so bad.

When she sat down in the water, she noticed how much sediment was rising up and making little brown clouds in the water. She managed to get clean, but only because of the shower. It made enough pressure to wash to dirt away, but it added a fresh layer of grit while she was showering. Each time she washed the dirt away, a little bit more would escape the pipe, and she finally reached a happy medium where she could get out of the tub. Dressed in her bathrobe with a tow-el around her hair, she went out to the living room to talk to Virgil about the dirt. She didn't want to start any problems, but she really wanted Virgil to address it.

"We have some dirt getting into the water."

"Oh, that explains why the coffee is so gritty. I just thought it was because I didn't know how to make it right."

Kelly took a deep breath and tried to explain without getting upset. "I'm surprised you didn't notice when you took a bath."

"I haven't bothered to take a bath yet," he answered.

Kelly stared at him, but the way he smelled made it clear that he hadn't showered in a week. It was getting more difficult not to get upset. "Why haven't you showered yet?"

"I just haven't felt that good lately," he answered.

I lost the baby, but he's the one feeling down in the dumps.

"So, where is this dirt coming from?" she asked.

"I don't know. It's getting too dark to go hunting around out there right now. I'll check it out in the morning."

He's right about that, it sure is getting dark. Not much either one of us can do in the dark.

"Please do," she answered. "I really need to get a hot bath."

After one last look at the pitch-dark night around her house, Kelly endured the half-dirty feeling and managed to get some sleep.

The next morning, Virgil headed out to the pipe and Kelly followed behind. He reached a place where some animal had dug a hole in the ground deep enough to put a crack in the pipe. It was only a couple inches across, but it was wide enough to allow dirt to fall through. Virgil covered it up with a small slab of rusting iron someone had left in the field, and it created a good enough seal for the time being.

Other people had left piles of gravel behind on the ground, stalks of grass shooting up between the rocks. Virgil had more than enough gravel to fill in the hole, and by the time he was done shoveling, the gravel was actually higher than the dirt around it.

"Up above this hill looks like a great place to build a house," he said.

It made Kelly feel better to see that Virgil was doing something about the problem. When she got back home and ran the water in the sink, she was surprised to see that it was actually running clear. She removed the shirt from the faucet and the bath water ran clear.

She took a nice hot bath that night, and the feeling of being clean was a huge relief to her. She turned off the faucet because the tub was filling up too much and leaned back into the hot water, closing her eyes and relaxing.

The water was warm enough that she fell asleep in the bathtub. When she woke up, the water was getting cold. She grabbed the showerhead, then remembered that the water needed to heat up first. She opened the tap full blast and a bullfrog fell out of the faucet and landed on her leg, pushed out by the water.

Kelly jumped up, screaming, while the bullfrog dropped into the hot water. It appeared to dislike the hot water, so he splashed his legs and plopped on the edge of the bathtub. From there, the agile creature turned around and leapt toward the toilet.

She screamed out loud, unable to control her panic anymore.

"Virgil! There's a frog in the bathroom!"

Virgil entered the bathroom. He didn't seem to notice that she was naked. His focus was on the floor.

"It's right there," she said, pointing. While Virgil scrambled around on all fours, muttering, she grabbed her towel and covered herself up.

Despite missing the first two times, he managed to get his hands around it on the third grab. The large animal bounced around inside his hands, but he held onto it and carried it outside, where it bounced off into the lilac bushes.

"There has to be another hole in that pipe somewhere," she said when he came back inside.

"I know," he answered. "There's no way it was inside the pipe the whole time."

Inside her mind, the image of the frog hiding inside the pipe took root. She could imagine other things living inside the pipe: lizards, snakes, and scorpions filled her imagination, and she shuddered at the thought.

"Thanks for giving me the creeps, Virgil," she said, unable to hide her sarcasm. Virgil seemed to ignore it, because he headed outside and grabbed the shovel.

When Kelly got dressed, she followed him outside. Whatever had dug in the dirt had also dug through the gravel, knocking the metal aside in its quest for water.

"It must have been a wolverine or something," said Virgil. "It made the crack even bigger to get at the water. Now I need to buy a new pipe. I've got to shut off the water valve at the spring, so it has time to dry out."

"But you'll be able to fix it tomorrow?"

"I'm doing my best, okay? It's still going to take some time for the pipe to dry out. Let me go shut off the water supply valve, and then we can get back inside. You know, I bought the land up on the hill too. This property goes all the way up there."

The next afternoon, when Virgil finally returned with the pipe and the glue, she thought it would be an easy fix. However, Virgil started digging the pipe up from one end to the other. When he had finally removed the old pipe, it didn't take him long to use the glue, but it took him until sunset to cover it all up.

"It's all fixed now," she said when he came in.

"Brand new pipe. Should last for decades."

"Thank you," said Kelly. "This should be much better."

Kelly was confident this time that things would go back to normal.

When nothing came out of the pipe at all, she started to get frustrated. She took the shovel herself and didn't even wait for Virgil. When she got to the pipe, she noticed the water leaking through the gravel at once. She didn't realize what hard work it was until she started getting into the rocks. The water poured out between the rocks, but it also pushed gravel out of the way, so she was surprised how quick it was done.

While she stared at the pipe already pushed two inches out of place, Virgil came up behind her.

"Well, shoot. Looks like the glue is on the wrong side of the pipe."

"How did you manage to do that?" she asked.

"It was really hard work, so I guess I got tired."

"Well, could you get un-tired and put the glue on the inside of the pipe this time?"

Virgil studied the pipe for a few moments. "I would, but it's still so wet that the glue won't stick. I have to turn off the valve at the spring again and let it dry up overnight. And look, it's getting dark already."

Kelly asked for patience, but it wasn't enough. "Another night without water. Just great." She walked inside, vowing to watch Virgil this time.

The next day, Kelly watched while he lined the inside of the pipe with glue and pushed it into place. Then he was able to sneak the other end into place after putting the glue on the inside and pushing them together. When he was done, both ends of the pipe were where they should be and the glue was drying.

"Now you can turn the water on?"

"No, it takes three hours for the glue to dry. That would be after sunset, so it would really be tomorrow."

"Okay, another night without running water. I guess that's all right. At least the glue will be nice and strong tomorrow."

"Once it dries, I'll cover the whole area so nothing else breaks through," answered Virgil. "I hope that this is the last time I have to fix those pipes."

The next day, Virgil finally opened the valve and Kelly watched the pipe sit in the ground. It refused to budge when the water entered, and the sound of running water was almost musical.

When she sat down in the bathtub, she felt four days of grime leave her skin, and she covered herself in soap three times. It was the first time she had felt true happiness in weeks, but she stayed wide awake in the hot water this time.

Chapter Eight

After getting clean, Kelly felt much more like herself, and a quiet evening with Virgil was the perfect ending to the day. With the plumbing fixed, she could get back to work on her stories. She had a wonderful idea about people that turned into lions at night, but that was all she had. When she tried to get into the story, she couldn't make the words appear.

While she worked on it, Virgil tried to interrupt her.

"We need to get some groceries," he said.

"Just a minute," answered Kelly. "I'm writing."

"That pencil hasn't moved in three minutes," he answered. "Let's get some food."

"Can't you go shopping by yourself?" she asked.

"I thought women liked to go shopping," he answered. "What's wrong with you? Are you depressed or something?"

"Maybe," she answered. "It's not like you'd understand how it feels to lose a baby."

"Hey, it was my baby too," he answered, and the venom behind the words reminded her how much pain he was going through. She put down the pencil and nodded.

"All right, you win, let's go shopping."

"That's more like it," said Virgil.

When they got to the grocery store, she remembered how fun it was to go shopping and started to enjoy herself again. She found the largest oranges she'd ever seen, and some apples that were fresh enough to last in the fridge for weeks. She also grabbed some potatoes, but when she was pulling them into the grocery bag, some of them got caught and went bouncing off the floor.

"Careful," said Virgil. "You're clumsy, aren't you?"

"A little bit," she answered.

"Well, if you weren't so clumsy, maybe you wouldn't have

fallen over. Just be more careful next time."

"Maybe you could be better at building stepladders next time," she answered. Virgil stopped complaining for a couple minutes, and she enjoyed the quiet moments when he was too stunned to have a good answer.

Kelly was glad he didn't flat out reveal what happened in the grocery store, but she still didn't care to be reminded of the awful incident. She was trying to put it out of her mind, but Virgil kept bringing it up.

"Just push the shopping cart. You can do that, right?"

"I was doing just fine, but accidents happen, you know that. Maybe I should be mean to you the next time you have an accident."

Kelly felt the insults that he leveled at her. Of course, she hadn't wanted to fall over. She just wanted to straighten out the picture. It wasn't really her fault.

Kelly took a deep breath and started pushing the grocery cart while Virgil added food to it. The pasta aisle had no other people in it, and Virgil headed in at once. He only got as far as the chili before he stopped and collected a couple cans from the shelf. After he put them in the cart, he stopped and thought for a few seconds.

"Do you want anything?" he finally asked.

"Yeah, I'm going to grab a couple of those Chef Boyardee raviolis."

Kelly stepped away to grab the cans from the bottom shelf.

"Where are you going?" snapped Virgil. "I told you to handle the cart." Frustrated, Virgil got two more cans of chili.

"It's not like you're the one that lost the baby," she muttered as she bent down to get the Chef Boyardee. She even grabbed a can of Spaghetti-O's for good measure.

As she started to get up, Virgil went red-faced with total rage. He threw one of the cans of chili at her feet while she was still rising so she had no time to react to the unexpected attack. The chili slammed into her foot, and the pain was bad enough that she cried out in pain.

"Don't you ever talk to me like that again!" Virgil shouted while she used her other foot to hop back to the shopping cart. She added her own cans while Virgil was busy with the one between the aisles. She grabbed the shopping cart handle with both hands and held on for dear life. She was expecting Virgil to strike her before anyone would show up to help her, but the attack never came. "That was going to be my little boy too," he said, and she saw some tears develop before he wiped them away. "I even had a little shirt for him to wear."

"But it was going to be a girl. Did you have a dress picked out too?" She meant it as an insult, but his answer shocked her.

"Yes, but now they'll never be used. I was thinking we could bury them out by the trees so we can have a proper funeral."

"You planned out a whole funeral? This really affected you, didn't it?"

Virgil nodded, and the tears in his eyes looked genuine enough to take all the fight out of her.

"So when we get home, we can have the service?" he asked.

"That sounds like a good idea," she answered. A funeral on the property made her shudder, but Virgil was already walking down the aisle. Kelly used the shopping cart for momentum.

"I still need some pasta," said Virgil. "Oh yeah, I need some sauce too." Before they left the aisle, ketchup and mayonnaise went into the cart. Virgil was cooperating with her now, and it seemed like he wasn't so angry anymore.

Kelly was surprised that no one else noticed the swelling in her foot as she headed to the checkout stands with Virgil. It was all she could think about as she stared at the floor. She managed to bump into another customer that was waiting in line, but the man didn't seem bothered. He even gave her a deep nod.

"That didn't even hurt," he said, which was a big relief to her, but she was more relieved that he wasn't angry with her.

Virgil was, though.

"Hey, I thought you said you could handle the shopping cart," he said. "Maybe I should just leave you at home next time."

Kelly didn't want to answer Virgil's comments anymore. Anything she said would just make her look worse.

"Don't worry about it, please," begged the man that she bumped into.

"That's easy for you to say, you don't live with her," Virgil snapped back. All the anger that Kelly thought she had shut down flooded back. Instead of getting ready to leave the store, Virgil looked like he was getting ready for a fight.

Kelly was astonished at the politeness the man showed. All he did was lean back with his arms crossed.

Kelly had seen her fair share of fights, but this one vanished into thin air once the gentleman refused to stoop to Virgil's level. She had expected the fight to begin at any moment, and adrenaline had already started to pump through her system. She still felt jittery, expecting some trouble to start again.

After Virgil got done checking out, Kelly started to push the shopping cart out of the store. Virgil got way ahead of her and out the sliding doors before Kelly could catch up to him. She kept pushing the cart at a slow pace, happy that Virgil was out of her way for a minute.

The man that she bumped into caught up to her, and she thought he was going to berate her now that Virgil was gone. Instead, he handed her a business card and calmly turned around and left.

Kelly hid the card in her pocket before she left the store, so she didn't get a chance to see what it said. As Virgil loaded the groceries, she sat down in the passenger seat.

She took a careful look at the card once she got into the car. It gave her the address of a domestic violence shelter, and no men were allowed, but since the man had a therapist's license, he was obviously part of the staff. She made sure to tuck the card away before Virgil got halfway done with the groceries.

As Virgil drove out of the parking lot, he asked, "What are you going to say when we're standing by the grave?"

"It's not something I had really planned out," she said.

"You're a writer. It should be easy," Virgil answered, and she wondered if he'd managed to forget what he'd done already.

While Virgil drove, the wind became violent. It battered the windows of the car, and Kelly noticed her window wiggling back and forth. By the time they got home, the dark clouds had started to peek over the mountain, and she knew that the first snow of winter was on its way.

Chapter Nine

Kelly thought she would make it through the funeral without crying, but the pain in her foot continued to bother her while they stood by the shallow grave.

It barely qualified as a funeral, much less a ceremony. No preacher read the eulogy, or anything like that. Virgil didn't even say anything when he picked up the box with the clothes.

Virgil had the clothing tucked into a white paper box, but she had a chance to see it earlier. The girl's dress was a hideous pink, and the boy's shirt was dark green, which would have at least covered any burping that would have occurred.

The idea that her baby would never get a chance to be burped was almost ironic to her at first, but it set off a torrent of emotions that she thought were already gone.

Virgil wrapped his arms around her in a sympathetic hug, and they both stood by the grave. She accepted his strong embrace and let the tension drain from her body. She could feel it descending, leaving her muscles, and she felt her muscles drift as well, deeper into his arms.

Virgil pulled her back up at once.

"You almost passed out, Kelly," he said. "Let's get inside."

Kelly wanted to correct him, but if he knew how she was feeling, he'd try to make love to her and try again. The doctor let her know that no more children were on the way, but Virgil wasn't going to understand that. She hadn't even tried to explain it to him yet.

The clouds got darker as they walked back, and the snow started to trickle out of the sky, tiny flakes at first, but big heavy ones by the time they got back to the house.

The sight of the first snowfall dotting the ground with innocent white was always a big deal for Kelly, and the wonder of the clean flakes felt like a release from the past they had put to rest.

She made tea when they got inside so she could be alone for a few minutes. Virgil sat down in the living room and fell silent. She thought he would be crying at the very least.

The long wait for the boiling water turned into a vacation from Virgil, so after she poured the tea, she stayed in the kitchen while it steeped instead of bringing it over to the living room. She studied the hypnotic trails of steam coming off the teacups and basked in the quiet moment.

"What's taking so long?" Virgil's voice interrupted, and she pulled the tea bags out at once and headed into the living room.

"Don't spill the tea," he said, and she was very careful not to let a single drop fall from the cups. "That's much better," he said, and took a long sip. He didn't even notice how she sat down in the chair extra fast. He also didn't notice her folded hands patiently sitting on her lap. His ignorance was no longer surprising, but it was still frustrating.

After a long silence, Kelly spoke up. "I'm going to do some writing," she said.

"Okay," answered Virgil, and Kelly put words on the paper. Some of the words—okay, most of the words, were totally random, but Virgil didn't have to know that. It just gave her a good reason to ignore him, and for some reason, he left her alone when she was writing, most of the time, anyway. This time, he left her in peace until he stretched his arms and headed to the bedroom. Kelly stopped writing once he went to bed. She closed the notebook and tucked it away so he wouldn't see the random words, but she waited a few minutes before heading into the bedroom.

He was fast asleep by the time she got into bed, and she was so relieved that he didn't wake up when she got between the sheets. All she had to focus on was going to sleep, and she was asleep at once.

Chapter Ten

The ice clung to the eaves of the house like an igloo, sheltering it from the wind and insulating it from the snow. Kelly got a beautiful dingo dog for Christmas, and it made her feel much safer. When Virgil would get mad at her, the dog would start to growl at once, and Virgil would have to calm down.

The dingo loved to run around in the backyard, but he was also good at digging through the snow. Kelly named him Houdini because he would crawl back under the fence when she came outside to correct him.

Virgil got a kitchen table, one that expanded because of a runner in the middle that slid in and out. It wasn't an ordinary Christmas present, but they didn't have a kitchen table, so they put it in place right away.

Bright chrome lined the side of the tabletop.

"That shiny stuff hurts my eyes," Virgil complained.

"It's lovely, Virgil. Just leave it alone."

Virgil waited only a day before adding a fresh coat of black paint to the edge of the table. Black was her least favorite color, but it had already found its way into the window trims and even the doorframe, so the streak of black around the table didn't surprise her. It was more of a disappointment.

Once the winter ended, the green plants returned.

Kelly still felt like something was going to go wrong, so when the bathwater never poured out of the tap, no matter how far she twisted the ancient handle, she felt vindicated for a moment.

Once the thrill of being right passed, the frustration grew at a fever pitch. She refused to put on her old clothes and dressed in a heavy shirt and thick pants instead.

"Get your shovel," she said as she headed out the door. "The water's not coming out again."

Houdini stayed by her leg as she walked out to the pipeline and only left her side to run over to the pool of water above the pipe. He started to drink the fresh water while Kelly waited for Virgil to catch up.

Water surged upward from the broken pipe, forming a swelling pool.

"I don't think a shovel's going to do it, Kelly," Virgil said once he caught up.

Houdini barked once at him in agreement.

"Would you go up there and shut off the valve already?"

"Okay, I'm going," he answered, walking up into the trees.

By the time Virgil made it back down to the pipeline, Kelly was already pushing the water out of the way with her shovel, swiping it back and forth.

"It would help more if you could clear some of the gravel, so I have more room for the bucket," he said.

"You don't even have the bucket yet," she answered.

"I'm going to grab it right now," he said.

Kelly started to work on the gravel, but the water kept sloshing the gravel off her shovel. She had to turn it upside down and scoop the rocks up out of the pool.

Virgil returned with the bucket and used his own shovel to help her. Their neighbor didn't feel like helping, though. He just watched them with a large smile on his face as he watered his window plants.

Kelly started to get even more frustrated at missing her bath, knowing that her neighbor still had running water. She kept shoveling even while Virgil was draining the water a bucketful at a time.

The hard work made Kelly feel warmer, and she got used to the rhythm of scooping the gravel before she heard the scrape of the metal pipe. She stopped digging and waited until Virgil could lower the water.

The pipe had a massive crack, two feet long.

"The pipe froze solid this winter. Now that it thawed, the pipe expanded and split apart."

"I thought you said you laid it deep enough," Kelly said.

"I thought I did too, but now I have to get a loan to pay

for new pipe," he answered with a whimper. Houdini answered with his own whimper. "Just get the rest of that water out of there."

"And where are you going?" she asked.

"To get the loan, and the new pipe. I'll be back soon."

Virgil drove off as Kelly worked on the rest of the water.
The bucket was too heavy for her to lift when it was full, but
she made good progress with the lighter shovel blade. She
lost track of time as she worked, until Houdini started whining and scratching her leg.

Houdini stayed close to Kelly as they walked back to the
house, but they were only halfway home when Houdini
stepped in front of her and blocked her.

"You almost made me fall over," she said in a firm tone.
"I want to get back inside."

Houdini gave a low growl, but Virgil was nowhere in
sight. She tried to shoo him forward again, but he kept
growling and staring down the path.

That's when Kelly noticed the rattlesnake stretched
across the path in front of her. It seemed to be just relaxing
in the springtime sun, but the deadly snake was still in her
way.

The rattler bobbed its head up and down, returning Houdini's growl with a high-pitched rattle. She started to realize
how much danger she was in as the standoff continued.

The snake shuddered louder, and Houdini growled. At the
peak of the conflict, the snake, still wiggling the tip of its tail,
slithered off the path and left her alone.

"Good boy, Houdini," she said. Once they made it back to
the house, Kelly gave the dog a treat. The idea that the rattlesnake could have bitten her scared her a lot, but it also
gave her a bit of a thrill. The narrow escape made her feel
more alive.

Virgil came back hours later, hauling the new pipe in the
back of the truck. He kicked some of the fast-melting snow
away from his path as he came inside.

"I'm going to start trying to be a handyman," he said.
"I've learned so much fixing this place up."

"You still want me to help with the pipe, right?"

"No, don't worry about it. Now the pipes have these
flanges, these big screws that go around the outside. I can

take care of it by myself."

"Well, that's a relief," answered Kelly. She didn't mind staying inside while he finished the work.

Hours later, Kelly still wanted to take a bath. When he came in, Virgil went straight for the kitchen and ran the water in the sink. It was an instant signal that the pipe was fixed. Kelly went into the bathroom to get started on her interrupted bath.

"There was a rattlesnake out there," said Virgil.

"I noticed the rattlesnake," she said. "You killed it, right?"

"Of course," said Virgil. "I did promise to protect you, remember?"

"You did make that promise, and I'm so glad you remembered."

"Once I start getting work as a handyman, it will be a lot better around here, I promise."

Houdini followed her around for the rest of the day, even lounging by the bathroom door while she took her bath.

Chapter Eleven

Kelly tried to write sometimes, but melancholy had taken over her mind. Over time, she had built the story of the ghost with no eyes, but the sadness brought writer's block, and the finishing touches just weren't there. It sat in her desk, waiting to be polished, along with other stories she didn't feel the energy to write anymore.

A short story contest had changed her mind, though. Virgil never bought the paper, but sometimes it arrived for free on Mondays when they were trying to get new subscribers. A company in Wisconsin was running a short story contest, and the winners would get cash as well as the printing of their story. It was the $200 cash that caught her attention. It was a chance to actually make something out of the work she'd done.

Virgil managed to keep the water running for a while, but even when he tackled projects inside the house, he didn't do very well. A leak started to cause dripping noises in the bathroom, and Virgil went on the roof three or four different times. After all of his work, the dripping water continued to hit the floor.

The horrible ping of the water hitting the tile interrupted her thinking and made the writer's block worse.

Kelly propped the pages up on her desk, making herself focus. She studied the writing in front of her, noticing something she could fix before the drip interrupted her. She put the pen against the paper and marked where she wanted to change. After the next drip, she changed the order of the words, and after the next drip, added a second verb for good measure so that the girl jumped and then tried to steady the flashlight in the same sentence.

The dripping sound started to go away while she worked.

When she was done polishing the manuscript, she started to retype the story from start to finish. She found a few more things to change, but she caught them in time before she typed them up.

When she was finally ready to send off the envelope, she got even more nervous than before. She noticed that her fingers were shaking when she closed the metal bracket on the manila envelope, and she was glad she had already written down the mailing address. She noticed that her tongue was dry when she tried to lick the stamp, and she ran her tongue across her teeth, trying to bring some moisture to the surface.

Kelly was sure that the $200 would bring more food into the house. The excitement brought her spirits up, and she tried to endure the intervening months before the answer came back.

While she was waiting for the letter, the rain got worse. Day after day, it pounded on the roof, and the leak got even worse. Pools began to appear in the front lawn, small gopher holes collecting the water. When it collapsed the gopher's house, the water would rush underground fast enough to leave bubbles popping to the surface. She knew that the field would have even bigger pools, so she went outside even though Virgil was still busy tinkering around on something in the bedroom. She didn't know what it was, but she could hear the hammering and tapping, so she knew it was something he was inventing. She didn't know what it was going to be, but Virgil had not made any successful inventions yet.

With everything considered, Kelly felt like she'd have a better chance selling her story than waiting for Virgil's invention to get done.

Kelly walked around the field to get inspiration, wearing a bright green rain poncho and carrying her umbrella. The raindrops kept muddying the surface of the pool, and the grass hovered beneath the surface, trying to reach for the air, not understanding where it went.

Each pool was bigger than the last, and she wondered where all the small pits came from. Some were almost round, but most were strange ovals, left behind from some ancient excavation project, perhaps, or dynamited away to reveal gold. Maybe the gold didn't reveal itself, and they moved on, leaving the cratered ground behind.

She couldn't find any rhyme or reason to the shapes of the pools, but she did notice that they were rising.

She walked all the way out to the pipeline and the spring, but the water was so generous that the spring was overflowing, gathering more rainwater than it could dispense.

She knew that repairs needed to be made to the side of the dam, but they would be impossible in this weather. The dam had never been designed to hold back this kind of water. It was merely a small dirt embankment meant to make the spring water a few inches deeper.

On her way back from the spring, the rain pounded so loud against the dirt that she felt her ears ringing from the sound. As she got closer to the house, she felt a sudden pain in her ankle, but she didn't think too much about it.

Two steps after the sudden pain, Kelly felt dizzy, worse than when she lost the baby. She noticed blood leaking out of her ankle from two small bite marks.

The dizziness got worse, and nausea punched her in the stomach, twisting her insides with pain until she cried out loud. She didn't know that she could suffer this much, and she tried to keep moving, but she had to drop to her knees before she could get to the house.

The pain almost stopped her movement, but she used her arms to push forward on all fours. She made it inside and tried to get into her chair.

Once she got to the living room, Houdini was by her side, trying to help her. He squared his shoulders, and she was able to get into the chair with his help.

Once she sat down, she started to catch her breath.

"Virgil," she said, but she knew her voice wasn't that loud.

Houdini ran off at once, banging away with his paw on the bedroom door.

"Knock it off," said Virgil as he came out. "Leave me alone. Don't jump on me."

"He's trying to get you to help," said Kelly as he came into the living room.

"Well, what's wrong with him?"

"He wants you to help me, Virgil, can't you see that?"

"Oh, you do look pretty pale," he said.

"I got bit by something when I was out walking around," she said.

"Let me see your ankle."

"Let me get my footrest up," said Kelly. She pushed the lever with all her strength, and the size of her ankle was surprising to her. She could feel the pain spreading around the bite, but the swelling made her foot look twice as big. Her shoe had already torn away, but she hadn't noticed it.

"You got bit by a rattlesnake," he said. "I know what to do about that."

Kelly was surprised that he was actually competent at something, but she was too happy to give him any sarcasm. When he cut the skin on her ankle without warning, she was not amused.

"That hurts really bad!" she shouted. "Are you sure you know what you're doing?"

Virgil put his mouth on Kelly's ankle and started to inhale forcefully, drawing the blood out of her ankle.

"Are you trying to drink my blood?" she asked, panicking.

Virgil spit the blood out of his mouth, spitting extra times for good measure. "I'm trying to get rid of the venom," he said. After another deep draw, he spit some more, and picked her up in his arms.

Virgil had never carried her across the threshold after their marriage, but now he carried her without comment out of the house. She noticed the threshold as they crossed it, and she thought about how romantic it was that Virgil was carrying her. She felt protected in his arms, and she felt sleepy. Her eyelids started to close.

"Keep breathing, Kelly!"

Kelly tried to take deeper breaths, but it was difficult.

"Don't tell me you're having an asthma attack. Didn't you bring your inhaler?"

Kelly gasped for air.

"Left at home," was all she could get out before she started fighting for air again.

Virgil pushed the car into a higher gear and sped down the city streets as fast as he could. He passed the other cars without a second thought as he raced to the hospital, but Kelly noticed that the other cars were barely moving.

He must be going really fast. I hope he doesn't get into a wreck on the way there.

Kelly didn't remember what happened when they got to the hospital. Everything was out of focus. When she woke up in the hospital bed, she could breathe much easier.

Virgil was sitting by her bed in one of the chairs. She hadn't expected to see him there, but he appeared concerned this time. She hoped that this would change his attitude toward her, but his silence spoke volumes.

When the doctor showed up, her mind was full of questions, but the doctor only answered one.

"You're very lucky, you know. The venom hit your ankle bone instead of your muscles. We were able to stop your asthma attack when you got here, but I think it was more of a panic reaction than the venom itself."

Kelly tried to make light of the situation, to make her mood a little better. Virgil still didn't speak.

"It was just a tiny rattlesnake," she said. "I think it was a baby."

"The younger ones have more venom than the adults," he answered. "Now I know you're lucky."

Virgil remained silent again, and it didn't help her mood one bit.

I might be lucky, but that rattlesnake bite still hurts really bad. At least the pain is a nice reminder that I'm still alive.

Kelly could tell that the anti-venom was working. It was strong enough to break through the blood clots caused by the rattlesnake poison, and she could feel her veins thumping as blood pushed through the blockages.

Chapter Twelve

At the mailbox, Kelly pulled out an envelope. She noticed the Milwaukee, Wisconsin stamp mark at once and opened the envelope in the front yard. She didn't have time to get inside before she started reading the letter.

"*Dear Kelly Barrett,*" the letter began, and then she knew it was about the story.

She stopped in her tracks, too excited to keep moving.

"*Underwood Publishers has decided to pass on your short story.*" The letter printed this decision in black letters, just like a standard response, but the whole thing was so formal that she just felt like she'd been rejected all over again.

It wasn't just the rejection from the company; it was a rejection against her, not just her story. She didn't know how to accept it, and her mind tried to shift into denial.

"Maybe I'll get accepted next time," she said out loud. "They just couldn't see how bright I really am."

"Get in here, Kelly! I need to see if the *TV Guide* got here."

Kelly looked through the rest of the mail. The precious *TV Guide* magazine sat among the mail in her hands.

"You know how much I love that crossword puzzle! Bring in in here right now. I haven't got all day."

Knowing that he wouldn't understand, Kelly went inside without mentioning the letter. After he went to bed, she took the rejection letter and pinned it up against the wall.

I'm trapped in this marriage. I'm trapped in this house. These rejection letters will put a staircase on the wall, and someday, I'll climb out of here. It doesn't matter how many times people push me down. I'm just going to keep getting back up again. This might be a difficult time, but the hard times won't last forever. I just have to keep going, just one foot in front of the other.

Resolved not to break down, Kelly sat down in her chair and started working on another story. It was about a woman whose window cracked in the dead of winter. She thought it would be a good start to a story, but the woman's desire to be young again seemed so crazy. She had no idea what to do with it, but she knew that it was better than nothing.

As she kept writing, she didn't notice what time is was until it was 3 in the morning and the full moon was past the middle of the sky. It hung over the Rockies, and Kelly wondered if she was ever going to escape.

Exhausted by the long night of writing, she fell asleep.

Chapter Thirteen

Year after year passed away while Kelly's wall grew one rejection letter at a time. The staircase became a series of columns, finally filling the wall edge to edge and dancing on upward. When they started to fill up against the ceiling, she started on the next column, but there was still plenty of empty space on the wall, waiting to be filled by rejection letters.

"What are you going to do when that wall fills up?" asked Virgil one day.

"Don't bother asking me that. I'll just start another wall. We have plenty of empty walls left."

"And we still have an empty house," answered Virgil.

Kelly remembered that day well, because her response surprised her.

"That's easy for you to say. I'm the one that can't have any children."

"You'll regret that," Virgil answered, and since then his touch had grown cold. It didn't matter what happened, she couldn't make his hands get warm. A darkness had settled over him, and he wasn't the same. The bitterness had left him empty inside, and his anger continued even if the insults stopped happening as much.

Kelly knew that plenty of space remained, but the encroaching stack of rejection letters continued to pile up and consume it. At some point, she would have to start on a second wall.

The other thing that happened after this particular rejection letter was one of the worst things she went through. She was sitting on a chair in the front lawn, trying to enjoy some time in the sun, when the ground under her chair leg gave way and a foot-wide hole opened up in the ground. Rocks went scattering down the tube and into the ground.

When Virgil finally came outside, she'd managed to pull the chair free, but the hole in the ground perplexed her.

"Someone had a well out here," Virgil said.

"Well, can't you cover it up? Someone could break a limb out here."

Virgil looked around to find something he could fill the hole with. He noticed the chair leg all twisted and stopped looking for a solution.

"What did you do to the chair?"

Kelly took a deep breath. "That could have been my leg. It went down into the hole."

"Once again, you can't even look underneath you when you put a chair down. You're really clumsy, you know that?"

"That could have been my leg," Kelly repeated, but it didn't seem to get through to him.

"I know!" said Virgil, hurrying over to a wide rock. "This ought to work, right?"

Kelly hoped that, for once, he was right, but the next morning brought the hole back to the front yard. The rock had already been moved away. She found it underneath a cardboard box that said "Moving Sale" a couple blocks away. She brought the rock back to the hole, but that was the least of her worries. Now she had to find something to cover the rock.

The front lawn had plenty of grass, and she had to wander to find enough dirt to cover the rock.

Kelly went back inside and tried to relax. She knew it was going to be a long day.

When her sister waved across the lawn, Kelly hurried outside.

"Don't go near the dirt pile," she said. "Somebody had a well over there."

"Come over here then. I wanted to get you some pastries."

"Really?" she asked.

"Come on, you mean you don't want maple bars anymore?"

A few minutes later, they were inside a café eating maple bars and drinking iced mochas.

"So, how are things going?" her sister asked.

With almost no one in earshot, Kelly felt much safer. "He's always bringing up the past, like the time I dropped that hammer on my foot." Kelly worked on a maple bar while she reacted. It would take a while.

Sarah's eyes opened wide, and she knew it wasn't the coffee. "Seriously? If you can move on from the bad things that happened in your past, so can he. Now he's just using it as a crutch. Don't tell me, he says you remind him of the past."

It was Kelly's turn to be shocked. "How did you know? I don't do a thing to trigger him, but he still goes back into the past to justify his anger, instead of being in the present moment."

"I know what mental abuse is. He's the one that chooses to behave like that. The choice of how to react is always yours. That's not what I'm talking about. Mom talked to that man from the domestic violence shelter the other day. She's worried about you too. He told her what happened at the grocery store. You didn't break your foot because you dropped a hammer on it. You broke your foot because he threw a can of chili at you. He mentioned that Virgil tried to start a fight with him."

"But if I wasn't so clumsy—"

Sarah interrupted her. "Don't think like that. You don't need to put yourself down too. Clumsy? You're just on edge, that's all. Is he still drinking?"

"Two beers every night, sometimes three." Kelly wanted to change the subject, but she went back to her negative thoughts. "He said that if I wasn't so clumsy, I wouldn't have lost the baby."

"Something horrible happened to you, but now he wants you to think that it's your fault. Can't you see that he's using these things against you? You can't be the victim and the perpetrator at the same time. It always takes two people."

Kelly refilled her cappuccino cup with some of the house blend. She didn't want another cappuccino because she'd be too wired, and then she'd be clumsier.

"You don't have to avoid it, Kelly. Just admit that you need help."

"I can't give up on him, Sarah."

"I can't give up on you, Kelly. Even Mom doesn't want to

give up on you. It just breaks her heart when she can see how much Virgil's been making you cry. She came over a couple weeks ago, but you were crying, and she just couldn't bear to talk to you."

Kelly remembered the incident, but she also remembered what caused it. While Virgil did make her cry a lot, that wasn't the reason she was upset that day.

"I'd just gotten another rejection letter, Sarah. It had nothing to do with Virgil."

Sarah still looked at her with concern. "Just think about it, Kelly. What if he does more than break your foot? How do you really know what he's capable of? What if he hits you in the head? What if I lose you?"

Kelly didn't answer right away. She ate a maple bar instead while the idea registered. If her sister was worried about losing her, she knew the danger had to be real. It was all the evidence she needed that her sister really cared about her.

"Sometimes, I just feel trapped," she said.

"I'm glad you're being honest," answered Sarah. "If you ever want my help, all you have to do is ask."

"One of these days," she said. "I promise you, one of these days, I'll get away from him for good. I'm just not ready."

"I'm always going to be here for you, Kelly, you know that."

Kelly nodded, but she wasn't able to make the next step, where she admitted that she needed help to escape a toxic relationship. Instead, she finished her coffee and went back to Virgil.

Chapter Fourteen

Twenty years later, Virgil and Kelly still had an old wooden coffee table with the runner in the kitchen, where Virgil was slouching. Hideous black paint still lined the edge, and Virgil still refused to cover it up. Cracks in the linoleum read like a crazy tic-tac-toe game. The kitchen was in desperate need of a renovation.

Sarah had moved away to Seattle two decades ago, despite promising that her door was always open. It was too long of a drive for Kelly to get to Seattle, but she always wondered what Sarah would do if she actually showed up.

Kelly's parents had moved overseas because it was a better place to retire and they didn't have to pay as much rent in Europe. Her father had always told her, "You made your bed, now you have to lie in it," even though he didn't take that advice himself.

Bush the younger occupied the Oval Office, and his stimulus packages kept the economy going, but it didn't seem to help her and Virgil. Poverty had become something she was used to.

As she waited for the hot water to boil, she counted the seconds between the drips under the sink. They syncopated with the drips in the saucepans scattered around the house.

One drip had managed to turn into several after Virgil applied tar to the roof. She'd seen him put the tar up there, and the bucket was empty when he'd come back down, so he had to have put it on the roof, but now it leaked more than ever.

When she poured the vanilla-flavored coffee crystals, the aroma lifted to her nose, calming her despite the chaos and muffling the drips. The familiar warmth from the mug warming her cold fingers and the pleasing smell gave her a momentary escape.

Even though Kelly and Virgil were about the same age, Virgil was getting a potbelly from the beers, and his hair had been slowly marching away from his forehead where it had once been thick and flowing.

"Are you writing again? Don't you know that's never going to go anywhere?" Virgil asked.

"I write every day," she answered.

"You've been promising to get one of those stories sold for years now."

He's just trying to get under my skin.

The knowledge didn't stop her from being bitter, and she'd gotten used to talking back over the years. "How about all the promises you made me? The big house on the hill?"

The argument had become a routine they both knew well. It had been a loveless relationship for many years. No matter what he did to humiliate her, she could never give up on her writing. It was as natural to her as breathing.

Virgil said, "I'll see you later, because I'm actually going to be working today. This guy I met, Doug, is putting me to work on some construction stuff."

"What, painting?" she asked. "That's about all you're good at. You're no good at plumbing or roofing, and anyone can plant a bush!"

"I can do odd jobs! I can nail boards in! This place is going out of business. They're a year behind. They need my help." Whenever Virgil tried to defend himself, he would start to squeak in higher and higher pitches, something that Kelly always found annoying.

"Yeah, I guess they'll take anyone they can get, huh?" asked Kelly. Virgil glared at her without answering. "I mean, the kitchen sink still needs to be fixed so it stops leaking. And the roof is leaking water every time it rains. Oh look, it's leaking now." A new leak had developed in the kitchen, and the floor was starting to get wet from the droplets hitting the linoleum, peeling it off the floor that much faster.

She walked over to the cupboard and opened it to find three pans left. The other pans were already on the floor, collecting water. "Great! Three more leaks and I'll have to buy more pans!" She grabbed one of the saucepans and put in on the floor to catch the water.

"You think I like it? I don't!" yelled Virgil. "I hate this roof! I hate this whole house. I wish we just had the money to tear it down and build a new one."

"Well, sometimes, you have to mend the things you do have rather than trying to go out and get new things. How did our ancestors survive when a bear destroyed their house?" Kelly crossed her arms, waiting for a good answer.

"They built a new one, just like I want to do," Virgil shot back.

"It would be nice if you would fix some things around this house once in a while!"

"I've been doing the best I can!" Virgil's coffee cup sailed across the room, already empty. Kelly ducked as it shattered.

"Now you know why I collect so many coffee cups!" Kelly was steaming mad. "Stop breaking my things!"

Virgil gave her a tired stare, paused for breath, and then just sat there for a few seconds. Finally, his gears started clicking again. "Writing's not a real job. You know your children's stories are never going to sell."

"Well, I'm not working at the library today, so I have to do something, don't I? Writing's my passion, you know that!"

Virgil changed the subject, because he realized he was losing the argument. "I've got to go. I don't want you to make me late on my first day of work!"

He headed out the door and Kelly yelled, "Don't slam the—" Then she flinched at the sound of the crash and covered her ears to protect them. Kelly finished her coffee, which was already getting cold.

She went to the bathroom to collect herself and wash her face, already sweaty from the morning's argument. She hated it when mornings started this way, more arguing and conflict. She had some wrinkles behind her eyes, and underneath them, but in spite of that, she still had to smile back at her face. Even though she admired herself, she knew Virgil didn't anymore. Today seemed like it was going to turn out just like any other day.

Kelly noticed the postmaster arrive, so she geared up her courage and headed outside. She tried to walk as fast as possible, looking back and forth, not feeling comfortable in her own front yard.

As she was going out to the mailbox, she noticed something red lying on the ground and she leaned over to pick it
up. As she did so, she became aware of Neil's presence next
door. The creep was staring at her again, same as usual. As
she picked the red object up, she recognized it as one of Virgil's tools, a wrench he usually used. He must have dropped
it, she thought.

As she was bending over to pick it up, she heard an off-
tune whistle coming from Neil.

"Nice ass!"

Kelly paused, and, looking back, she noticed he was still
gawking at her. She grabbed the wrench and rose back to
standing.

As she walked to the mailbox, she allowed herself one
quick glance back at Neil, and then shrugged her shoulders,
smiled, and waved, because that's all she could do anyway.
No matter what she did, he would keep staring at her. The
pervert's window was hanging open, but it wasn't hot enough
to leave the windows open yet, so he was just costing himself more on his heating bill. Raindrops fell through the open
window, but Neil never moved to close it.

He seemed reassured by the eye contact, because he
started talking to her again. "Hey! When are you going to
mow that lawn of yours?"

"When I win my first million, I'm filling up the tank on the
lawnmower. It's out of gas." She looked across the lawn,
feeling compelled to ask him a sarcastic question. "Hey, do
you have any gas money for the mower? Or were you thinking of charging me for the service?"

"Well, for a good-looking woman like yourself, I'll do it for
free!" he called back. The weirdo broke into a strange cackle
that reminded her of the old men in nursing homes. It made
her shiver with revulsion.

"No, thank you, that's fine, thank you for offering," Kelly
said, and she continued down the driveway, trying not to
look as creeped out as she really was.

Neil kept on staring at her anyway, and grinning, all the
way down to the mailbox. She got to the mailbox, looked
inside, and found an envelope addressed to her.

More focused on the envelope than her neighbor, Kelly
walked back inside. She heard Neil shouting behind her. "I

hope the letter's not some love letter from one of your boy-friends. That would make me real jealous."

"Not a chance in hell!" Kelly didn't bother to turn around to shout at him. She was getting too mad to even look at him anymore. She knew every detail of him, his horny, leer-ing eyes, his poorly trimmed beard that made him look even worse. She had to watch his disgusting face every time she walked to her mailbox.

She set the letter on the writing desk once she made a fresh cup of coffee. The desk was empty except for an old Underwood typewriter with a missing S key that she found at a thrift store. She'd never had enough money to get a com-puter. She sat down and opened the envelope.

The letter read,

Dear Kelly, we regret to inform you that Black Hawk Press has decided not to accept your story, "The Fox and the Crow," for publication. Although someone else might find it acceptable, it's just not the story for us. We wish you good luck in your future.
George Hendricks, Black Hawk Press

After she read the letter, she leaned back in the chair and buried her face in her hands.

"Another one! It never changes! It's so unfair! I'm putting you up there with the others."

Each time she sent a story off to the agents, it was with the hope that she would be delivered from here and finally afford a nice place to live, where the ceilings didn't leak. But every time she got another rejection letter, it would just mo-tivate her to work harder.

Recovering from her frustration, Kelly calmly picked up the letter and carried it over to the far wall of the room. She put the letter in her hand up, pulled a thumbtack out from further down, and tacked the newest letter in place. Now the wall was almost completely full.

Kelly sat down in the chair and drank some coffee, look-ing at the letters. The more she thought about it, the angrier she felt, frustration consuming her once again. She decided the only non-destructive thing she could do at this point was write another story. Kelly walked away from the wall without saying a word and sat down at the table with the typewriter.

The only time she was truly happy was when she was writing children's stories. It allowed her to escape into another world, one without creepy neighbors or husbands that got worse and worse every day. Her world was going to have dogs, and cats, and talking squirrels too. As she sat there, thinking about the talking animals, she began to come up with a story. Being rejected over and over again made her feel like a freak. It made her feel like she was missing something important, as important as a tail was to a dog. As she thought about dogs' tails, inspiration struck.

"Once upon a time," Kelly said as she began writing, "there was a little dog that didn't have a tail." After she got done with that part, she saw a fly land by the typewriter. The flyswatter was hanging on the wall in front of her, and she grabbed her favorite weapon. Kelly suddenly felt justifiable rage leap up inside her and she took all her aggression out on the fly, reducing it to a ball of gray sludge underneath her flyswatter. Then she returned to typing.

"The dog was so sad that she didn't have a tail like the other dogs," she said out loud as she wrote, pausing every time she needed an S.

Chapter Fifteen

Kelly had just introduced a long-haired Maine Coon cat named Lucy to her story when she looked up at the clock and realized that Virgil would be home in a few minutes. She went to the kitchen, quickly turned on the oven, then opened two cardboard packages and tossed two Banquet dinners inside. She sat down to wait for his arrival, laying out the silverware like it had been on the table all day.

Her phone rang and, to her surprise, it wasn't Virgil. It was her sister, Sarah, calling from Seattle. "Hey, Sarah, how are things over there?" she asked.

"Oh, you know, just like Montana, but even rainier."

Kelly laughed. "It's springtime over here, less snow than winter. How's your husband?"

"Oh, he got a traffic ticket last week, but I wanted to see how you and Virgil are getting along." Sarah sounded concerned, so Kelly decided not to tell her how bad things were really getting. She felt a deep stab of pain when Virgil's name came up. His resentment was a wound that stayed close to the surface.

"Well, you know how he is," Kelly answered. "He's always working hard. Who am I kidding? He hardly works at all. I mean, he has a job, but it hardly pays him any money at all, and it takes him forever to get each project done. I keep getting rejection letters, too. I even got one today." Kelly hadn't meant to reveal that last detail, but she realized that she couldn't keep up a false front forever.

Sarah was quiet on the other end of the phone for a few seconds, but Kelly could hear her eyelashes prick up as her voice came chirring through the line. "Well, don't worry, Kelly. That just means it's not right for them. You'll find plenty of agents who want compassionate children's stories to hit the mainstream market."

Kelly loved talking to her sister, but she suddenly remembered she was cooking dinner. "Oh, sorry, Sarah, but I've got to take off. I'm baking lasagna and Virgil is never late for that."

"Well, you take care of yourself, my sister," said Sarah before hanging up.

Virgil came home and walked in, leaving the front door hanging open—as usual. Kelly hated that so much and he did it at least twice every day. Every time he did, more happy flies buzzed in. Kelly asked him, raising her voice, "Do you mind closing the door? Flies get in here! I had to kill ten of them."

"Well, the sooner you can get out here, the sooner I can close the door!" Virgil answered. He didn't wait for an answer. "Get in the Blazer! I've got a surprise for you!"

Kelly groaned. "Right now? But I already have dinner in the oven." Kelly didn't care for Virgil's idea of surprises. They never worked out good for her. For example, the stepladder had been a surprise, and so had the well in the front yard.

"Turn the oven off! There's something I want to show you!"

Kelly got up, turned off the oven, and followed him into the Blazer. Without warning, he took off into the field by their house. The Blazer bumped and rattled. He turned towards the hill without warning and began going straight up the very steep incline behind their house.

"Are you crazy?" she screamed. Her hands were clenched on the dashboard. Her fingers were gripped so tightly the blood was rushing away from her hands and her fingers were turning as white as the bones inside. As they went higher and higher, she thought they were going to make it, but soon enough, there was a deafening crunch and the Blazer stopped. They were caught on something big. The Blazer rocked and it felt like it was going to tip over.

"Now what are you going to do? We're stuck!" yelled Kelly.

She started to shake. Her heart was pounding, and she was losing her grip on the dashboard because her hands were starting to sweat.

Virgil gave a sarcastic laugh. "Just relax! You know I'd

never hurt you!"

"You're going to get me killed one of these days," said Kelly over the roar of the engine.

"Not yet," he answered. The axles started whining and the transmission emitted grinding sounds.

The tires screamed with fury as they spun against the ground. Dirt and rocks flew up behind the car as she looked in the rearview mirror. She looked in front and smoke was pouring from engine.

"That's smoke coming out of the engine. The car's on fire!"

"That's just steam from the radiator. Calm down, Kelly. You should be enjoying this!"

She gaped at Virgil in disbelief as he kept pumping the gas. "We really are stuck."

"No, we're not stuck!" Virgil yelled back. "Watch this!"

There were two loud crunches behind her and the Blazer took off again up the hill, finally clearing the top and shooting off down the field until it rolled to a stop. Virgil was laughing hysterically. She let go of the dashboard and forced open the door, allowing her to exit the car.

She staggered away, hands on her knees and catching her breath. She wiped her tears away before she turned around, then she felt secure enough to turn back and face Virgil, who was still laughing in the driver's seat and coughing from the smoke coming through the vents.

"What are you doing? Are you trying to kill us?"

Virgil grabbed the cold water from the backseat and started pouring it all over the engine. "We'll just give it a few minutes to cool off." Walking away from the clouds of steam, he grabbed her hand and started walking her through the field. "No, honey, that's not what I was trying to do. I just wanted to show you where I'm going to build the new house. I figure it will only take about two, maybe three, years to get all the money saved up! And look at the view! What a great view of the Rockies, huh? We're going to live right here."

Kelly didn't even bother to look. She could see them just fine from the house at the bottom of the hill. The Rocky Mountains stood high above them, across the valley, while far away in the distance, other mountains loomed. People flocked to Montana to see the Rockies, but to Kelly, the mountains were a force she could not conquer, keeping her trapped in this horrible life with Virgil.

Kelly's marriage to Virgil had been one long list of broken promises. She looked at him, and he was smiling like a goof. Kelly knew that Virgil meant well, but her heart sank because she knew the house would never be built.

"I don't have time for this crap! Don't make any promises you can't keep. You've been promising me a new house for years. Now I have to get back down there and finish cooking your dinner!" She started off towards the hill on foot. After several pathetic grunts, the engine finally turned over, much to her surprise, and Virgil backed up to talk to her again.

"Come on, honey, get in!"

"Not on your life!" she shot back, not even looking at him.

"Oh, come on, honey, I promise I'll use the road this time!"

"No you won't," she said. Kelly walked down the more level section, but Virgil didn't follow her. She looked behind her and Virgil was actually driving to the flat section, instead of risking his life going back downhill.

At dinner, Virgil tried to talk to her some more. "Hey, honey, guess who I met at work today?"

Kelly was still mad at him. She looked up, but only for a second before returning to her food. "Who?"

"I met a kid." To Virgil, a kid was anybody under 40. After that, Virgil continued to go on and on and on without ever getting to the point. Kelly tuned him out, and it was like the volume went down on his voice until she could barely hear him.

"Now that I'm working for Doug Carlton, I'll be making all sorts of money. His parents are rich too. He's been a contractor for years. He's got lots of projects he's working on."

After that, she started to tune him out. She knew it wouldn't lead to anything anyway. Virgil had an interesting way of going from job to job. No matter how simple the job was, he'd always find some way to ruin it so he couldn't work there anymore.

Later on, after she had finished eating and gone off to write for the evening, Virgil continued to laugh in a strange way towards the TV. It sounded like a chipmunk caught in a washing machine. Kelly wondered if his laugh was part of the problem with his jobs. She wrote a few more lines in the story before she wondered, *Is this all my life is going to be? Why can't one of the agents like my stories? It's got to get better sometime.*

She finished the story that night, but Virgil didn't seem interested, so she kept it to herself.

Later on, when they were having sex, she stared at the ceiling. She just wished Virgil would hurry up already. He had developed the habit years ago of pawing at her during sex, but every time he touched her that way anymore, it just made her cringe. At one time, she couldn't wait to feel his hands on her body at night.

After he finished, she smiled at him and he got off of her. He rolled over and fell asleep. It was one of the most annoying things about him, but at least she didn't have to listen to him panting anymore. Only quiet snoring emerged from his lips.

She rolled over and looked at the clock. It read 11:05. She kept staring as the minutes rolled by, thinking about tomorrow. Tomorrow would be a good day. Tomorrow, she would be reading to the children at the library. She closed her eyes, imagining their faces lighting up as she read her stories and the way they would jump up and down and laugh when she acted out parts of it.

Chapter Sixteen

Kelly always had a ritual before she went to the library. After a long, relaxing bath, she would get into her best clothes. She only had two nice outfits. Virgil never bought her any new clothes for her birthday. In fact, he didn't even buy her clothes as Christmas presents. She always got pots and pans and brooms, stuff like that.

Most of her clothes came from the Bozeman Goodwill, but every once in a while, a nice dress would come through and she'd get there early enough to grab it.

Today, she was in a red dress with a blue hem. She had looked through her shoes, but only one pair was presentable; the rest suffered from cracked leather while one pair didn't even have shoelaces.

She was about to get into her single pair of decent shoes when Virgil said, "Hey, Kelly! I want you to come out and meet somebody!"

She hurried to get into her shoes, but the more she hurried, the harder they were to slip on. She jammed her heel into the shoe painfully and walked out of the bedroom, surprised to see a handsome young man in the kitchen, standing quietly, not drinking a beer or anything, unlike Virgil's usual friends. "Hey, this here's Doug. I wanted you to meet him."

"I've got to get to work, Virgil. Remember, this is one of my days at the library? Tammy's waiting for me; this is not a good time." But she stood there for a few more seconds to look at Doug.

He looked like he was about twenty-eight or twenty-nine, but he had these ridiculous hundred-dollar cargo shorts on that just screamed rich kid and made him look even younger. She noticed that Doug, unlike Virgil, didn't have a lot of hair on his legs. He almost looked like he belonged on the cover of one of those exotic magazines, with his well-trimmed goatee and piercing eyes. He had a sharp jawline that he kept all the sideburns away from so people would notice. She realized she'd been staring too long and that she needed to say something.

"Well, it's nice to meet you, Doug."

Doug smiled at her. Kelly smiled back.

Virgil noticed how Kelly was acting and that Doug was looking back. To make a statement, Virgil came over and kissed her. She looked at him in surprise. She had always expected him to get jealous sooner or later, but the timing still surprised her. She returned the kiss, but the mere touch of his lips disgusted her.

"Virgil?" she asked. "Can I have the keys to the Blazer now? You don't want to make me late for work, do you?"

Virgil quickly fished the keys out of his pocket. "Don't forget to pick me up at four-thirty," he said. "The job site is right behind the Lakeshore Hotel."

Traffic on the way to the library was terrible. Some idiot in a big truck turned right in front of her, and she had to screech to a halt. When she stopped the Blazer, the engine died. She knew Virgil had damaged the engine when it gave up. She waited a few seconds before turning the key again, and the engine groaned as it turned over. When the engine finally kicked in, she honked her horn, but the truck driver was long gone.

"Darn it, Virgil! Now I'm going to be late. What were you thinking?"

The library had a nice green lawn and a parking lot, but there were only a couple cars there. Not too many people were there in the afternoon. The library itself was wonderful, the pride of Bozeman, and one of the first modern buildings to grace Montana.

The building ran on wind power, which she thought was a good idea, because it was almost always windy there, and cold in the wintertime. The roof always made her feel like she was floating. Three stories of windows allowed light to pour into the building during all seasons.

As she went inside, the light turned the pages of the books on the tables a shade of gold, and she wondered if old Midas himself was at work. She had a flash of imagination where she could see a book with pages made of solid gold. Her imagination then placed her name on the cover of the book.

Row after row of bookshelves proceeded until the wall that separated the library from the performance room, where there was a grand piano that she only wished she could play.

Tammy was waiting for her at the front desk by the time she got there. Her long blonde hair with dark highlights was always worn falling around her shoulders.

She was starting to get chubby, but that was useful in the winter months. She was in her mid-30s, and she always wore thick glasses with blue frames that couldn't dent her smiling personality.

A cart full of books was also waiting for her to shelve.

"Hey, Tammy."

Tammy smiled brightly. "Good afternoon, Kelly. Any luck with the publishers?"

"No, just another rejection letter." She shelved a boring science textbook nearby, and then looked for the right place for a book about penguins.

Tammy shook her head sympathetically. "I just don't understand it. You write such good stories. You're always making the children laugh."

Kelly had always imagined a life with children, but it had not happened for her. "I wish I could have children. But when I was younger, I had an infection in my ovaries, and it doesn't look like I can have children because of it. He's never managed to get me pregnant, and the doctor said it's unlikely after the infection left scars on my ovaries and damaged my eggs. But it doesn't matter, because he behaves like an animal in bed anyway." Kelly added a book on global warming to the shelf.

"Not all men are animals in bed, Kelly, and I hope you find someone that will take care of you. Sex isn't just about making babies, Kelly, it's more about feeling fulfilled and satisfied emotionally. That's what I think you really need, someone to satisfy you."

"The kids will be arriving soon," she said, shelving a book on warthogs.

Tammy smiled. "You've noticed the parents that listen to the stories too, right? You know that I listen to your stories at story time also. I've been trying to keep you positive, and you've made that story time into a real happening down here. One of these days, I'm sure you're going to get an agent to sell your stories."

"I wish I had as much hope as you do," answered Kelly, shelving another book. "Yesterday, I got another rejection letter. I keep going, but it would be nice to get one book published at least."

Tammy laughed out loud. "Publishers are like men, Kelly. One of these days, you'll run into a publisher that knows how to treat you right, and they will publish all your books; don't worry about that."

Kelly laughed at the analogy too. "They are just like men, Tammy. They don't tell you what you're doing wrong, just how they don't want to spend any time on you."

"You know, all the comic book people rejected Stan Lee for years until he got his big break? They said *The Incredible Hulk* was immature and cheesy. But they were wrong, weren't they?"

With a book on zebras, Kelly got done with the science section. She smiled in agreement. "Tammy, I don't know what I'd do without you. You keep me going. Which section should I do next?"

"The young adult books."

Shelving was a tedious process, but one she would happily do for the rest of her life. Every time she shelved a book, she thought about her own stories and how she would find a publisher someday.

Over in the YA section, the books all had to be arranged by last name of the writer. Every time she pushed another spine into place, she wished it was her name typed in black computer letters on the side of the book for easy reference.

"Barrett, Kelly," she said out loud.

It would look so nice. She continued to daydream as she filed books.

Tammy walked into the same section while she was doing her work, taking the time to ask her some questions.

"What's the deal with Virgil now? Shouldn't you just leave him or something? Why do you keep letting him bring you down?"

"It's just his heart. I'm terrified of breaking it. I can't bear to break his heart, even though he broke mine several times."

Tammy didn't bring it up again that day, but it was just as well because a couple of the little girls were arriving earlier and earlier. One girl arrived ten minutes early, but she went over to the children's section, followed by another one five minutes early. She thought it was wonderful that children were starting to show up early for her story times. If they showed up for her stories, she figured, they would definitely show up for interviews and other things where showing up early would be very important.

When she heard the children laughing as they entered the library for storytelling time, she stopped daydreaming. She loved the sound of little children laughing. It made her day brighter.

As she heard more of them piling in the door, she left the Young Adult section and turned around the corner to meet all the children. "Mrs. Barrett!" they cried out. "Read us a story!"

Kelly beamed at them. "Well, follow me then to the story room, because it's story time!"

The kids all yelled, "Story time!" one after another and started running for the story room.

"No running!" she said sharply.

"Sorry, Mrs. Barrett," they said, and slowed down. Kelly followed them.

Years ago, some of the children had been assigned a creative project, and when they were done, they had painted huge pieces of cardboard in bright colors. They had a castle, a big blue moat, a bunch of trees called the Enchanted Forest, and several characters from fairy tales.

Kelly got to the pictures and immediately had the house, some dogs, and the cat sitting against the wall, ready to tell her story. She sat down in front of all the children and said, "Are you ready?"

John, one of the older kids, said, "We're ready."

"Okay then, quiet, children, and I'll tell you a story. It's called 'The Dog with No Tail.'" All the children giggled.

Kelly spent some time removing the leather tail from the small dog. She squeezed her face in concentration as she removed the tail and the children giggled. Then she set the dog back down against the felt wall and the children quieted.

She read from her story in front of her as she moved the different figures to dramatize her story.

"Once upon a time, there was a dog with no tail. The poor little thing didn't like it. He didn't look like the other dogs. The other dogs laughed at him. He ended up being very shy."

"Why aren't there any pictures?" asked Daniel, one of the younger children in the audience. He poked at her sheet of paper, pulling it away from her.

"Please don't interrupt, Daniel. I'm sorry, but these are stories I created to read to you. They're not in picture books yet. Where were we?"

Daniel had to think for a few seconds. She used the time to pull her sheet of paper back.

"The dog was very shy, Mrs. Barrett."

"The dog was very shy because the other dogs would make fun of him." Kelly puffed out her chest and put her hands on her hips to imitate the bigger dogs. "Tail-less!" she said in a deeper voice. "No tail, no tail!"

The kids laughed and clapped as she strutted around in front of them, making it a funny activity. As she continued the story, she introduced the cat, the one that helped the dog with no tail stand up for itself. She kept pretending to lick her hand, grooming herself like a cat, and the kids giggled every single time she did it. She used the puppets to tell the story as well from time to time, and she heard lots of laughter and giggles from the children.

After the story was done, she read a couple of older folktales, and then story time was over. The parents were all showing up to get their children, and everybody left, except for her and Tammy. As she got done with work, she had the sinking feeling she got every time she was done and had to go home to Virgil. She tried to shake it off by buying some groceries.

As she was checking out, the older lady at the checkout stand told her, "Oh, I'm sorry, ma'am, but you only have fifteen dollars on your card."

She realized Virgil was, once again, spending money without telling her about it.

"Well, this is embarrassing. Now I have to put stuff back." As she returned the jerky and the peanuts to bring the cost down below fifteen dollars, she muttered under her breath, "Damn him! Does he want me to starve?"

The way he spent money on things like beer when she needed the money for groceries always ruined her day. Every day he seemed to be satisfied with his nightly beer, but if he didn't have it, he would be even more bitter and frustrated.

As she got out of the store, boiling with rage against Virgil for not being any help, she realized the sun was sinking lower and hurried back to the car.

Chapter Seventeen

Kelly opened the mail one package at a time after an uneventful dinner. She was too mad to say anything to him. But afterwards, she was going through the mail and found a letter from Ridgewood and Sons Publishers.

Kelly opened the envelope, expecting another rejection letter, but to her surprise, she discovered ten sheets of paper, all stapled together, with the name of her book, "The Fox and the Crow," on the front page.

She had never seen a contract before. She was very excited as she dived into the typed-up document. First it described the agreement and the marketing arrangements, such as book signings. Then it described how she would be assigned an illustrator that would make pictures for her book. After that, she learned about the 60% of each book sale she would be earning as a royalty, along with an advance payment of fifteen thousand dollars that would be hers once she signed the contract and mailed it back. Kelly was still trying to read through all ten pages of the contract when Virgil emerged from the bathroom with a belch and headed into the living room, a cold beer already in his hand.

Virgil sat down in his chair beside her, but Kelly was hoping that he would leave her alone. "What are you looking at?"

"This is a contract to get my book published."

"A contract? Let me see that!" He studied the contract with darting, venomous eyes. "This is a fake. These people are just ripping you off! You don't need this!"

"But it's a fifteen-thousand-dollar advance. Virgil. I actually do need this!"

Virgil was not going to be swayed.

"Kelly, if you take that advance money, then they won't give you anything until you sell, I don't know, five thousand books. It's just a kid's story. They can't charge fifteen dollars for it, you know. At the best, it's going to be five dollars, and then you're only getting three bucks, that is, after the advance is paid back. These contracts are complicated, and you have to read the whole thing before you make a decision."

Before Kelly could stop him, Virgil tore up the entire contract, all the pages at once, until nothing but a pile of shreds lay on the floor.

"But I wasn't done reading it yet, Virgil! Why did you do that?"

"Just trying to protect you, honey," he said.

She fell to her knees, heartbroken and sobbing. Kelly went from elated to depressed in a few seconds, and the fall was excruciating. When he tore up the contract, she lost hope in the future, and she started to feel despair.

"I'm just looking out for you, Kelly. You know these people are all rip-offs, every last one of them. I'm getting tired, I'm going to bed."

Kelly had a suspicion that he was regretting his decision and didn't want her to yell at him. It was more than a suspicion, because she'd lived with him long enough to know his behavior. He would probably try to be nice to her when she came to bed, because it would be his way of apologizing. Kelly had no motivation to forgive him, though, and she knew he'd made a mistake assuming that she would do so.

When Virgil left for the bedroom, Kelly started to pick up the shreds of the contract, sniffling. She put them in a box. After she had the paper collected, she buried it in the backyard so Virgil wouldn't find it, still determined to find a way to get even with him, but not having a clear idea of how.

That night, Virgil was reading a story to Kelly in bed. When he was nice enough to read her stories, it helped her fall asleep. This time, he was reading a Tom Clancy book to her. She kept her eyes closed and relaxed. It was hard to do, after all the things he did to hurt her, but somehow, she managed.

While her eyes were closed, the world was a safer place. She didn't have to see Virgil, just listen to the sound of his droning voice as it slowly put her to sleep. In spite of his emotional abuse, he always seemed to be more polite after the sun went down. As she was about to drift off into her dreams, she heard Virgil whispering to someone. "Shh! Be very quiet. Don't disturb my wife. She doesn't like you."

Bleary-eyed, she asked, "Huh? Did you say something?" She opened her eyes and looked down in shock at the end of the bed. Next to his slippers, standing on its hind legs and paying close attention to Virgil, was a large mouse. He was waving his front paws around in the air with excitement, doing that horrible little grunting-squeaking sound. "What in the world is that?" Kelly asked, hoping that she was still dreaming.

"Oh, that's Hector, my new pet. I've been reading to him for a few days now. Isn't he cute?"

"That's not a pet, Virgil! That's a mouse!"

"So? A lot of people keep mice as pets!"

"Not in their bedrooms they don't! Set a mousetrap and be done with it! Shouldn't that thing be in the backyard?"

"You know how much I care about animals, honey. I can't stand to see them starving out there."

"But they carry diseases, you know that, right?"

Virgil grabbed an empty mayonnaise jar, scooped up the smelly rodent, and carried it outside. "Just trying to make you happy," he added when he came back. "Goodnight."

Kelly got no sleep that night. Every scratch and creak sent chills down her spine, and she wondered how her life had gotten this bad. She felt something touching her leg, and she panicked, reaching behind her, but it was just Virgil's hairy legs.

The next evening, she thought everything would go back to normal. But after falling asleep, that squeaking sound woke her up again. She looked at the end of the bed, confused, not seeing the mouse anywhere. She got out of bed, noticing that Virgil was still awake. She could see the mouse on his side of the bed. Virgil was dropping cheese crackers down on the floor. The filthy rodent was leaving crumbs behind in his haste to grab them.

"What do you think you're doing? That mouse should be in the backyard. Did you ever hear of Hantavirus?"

"But it's my pet mouse, Hector. I've been reading to it every night for a week now."

"A whole week that thing has been in here? Well, you can keep reading to him all you want, because I'm sleeping in the living room!"

Kelly didn't expect to spend the whole night on the couch, but Virgil hadn't changed his mind. She felt a sharp pain in her foot in the middle of the night, but she didn't think too much of it. When she woke up, she found four little bite marks just above her ankle and they were swelling and turning red.

"That awful mouse bit me," she said out loud. Her voice was crackly, and her tongue couldn't find any moisture in her mouth at all. Her whole body ached, and a red line was crawling up her leg. She could see it moving, but it also weaved from side to side. She noticed the carpet fibers weaving from side to side too.

Kelly got dressed, but her muscles refused to cooperate when she tried to tie her shoes. She slipped some sandals on instead and headed outside. She planned to walk to the hospital, but it was getting hard to breathe and she didn't know why.

The Deaconess Hospital was not far from her house, but the walk took longer than it should have because she kept having to sit down and catch her breath. No one seemed concerned that she was having trouble. She made it to the hospital without anyone helping her.

When she got to the emergency wing, it was even getting hard to talk.

The receptionist looked very concerned when he sat down at the computer.

"I got a bite on my leg," she said, but her voice was deeper than before.

"When did you notice the bite?" he asked.

"This morning," she answered.

"Hmm?" asked the receptionist.

She hadn't realized how much the dry mouth was affecting her.

"This morning," she repeated, slower.

"Can I get your name?" asked the receptionist. "I need to pull up your file."

"Kelly Barrett," she said.

"What did you say?" he asked.

Kelly didn't bother repeating herself. She reached in her pocket for her driver's license. She handed it to the receptionist, and he started typing.

Kelly felt an alligator clip slide over her finger.

"Her blood oxygen saturation is down to eighty-five percent, her eyes are bloodshot, and her skin is jaundiced. This is a serious case," said one of the nurses.

Kelly felt pressure around her arm. She looked down and noticed a black bag filling up with air. "What's going on?" she asked.

The nurse didn't react to her question, but when the bag deflated, she nodded. "Her blood pressure is terrible," she said, but Kelly didn't understand the meaning. "Did she walk here?"

"Yeah, she was walking across the parking lot. Someone almost ran over her."

"So she has delirium from the hypoxia. Where's the driver of the car?"

"Right over there," said the nurse, pointing. "It gave the driver the fright of his life."

Kelly looked where the nurse was pointing, but nothing registered in her mind except for the concern written all over his wide-eyed face.

I don't remember that man.

Someone put an oxygen mask in front of her mouth. She took a deep breath of the cool air and felt an elastic strap slide into place behind her neck.

"That hurt," she said. A moment later, the tension on the strap was released and she felt better.

"Are you finished?" asked the nurse. "She needs to be in a bed."

"I've got her file pulled up," answered the receptionist. "Put your hand out for me." Kelly extended her hand, and the receptionist snapped the wristband closed.

Her chair slid backward, and she looked down and noticed the wheels.

"When did I get into a wheelchair?" she asked the nurse.

"About five minutes ago," she answered.

"How long have I been here?" she asked.

"That doesn't really matter, does it?" answered the nurse. Kelly thought she was irritated at her. "You should have been here hours ago."

"I came in as soon as I woke up," she answered.

"You're probably alive right now because you woke up," said the nurse, and she felt much better because she didn't want to make the nurse upset.

When Kelly got to the room, the nurse made a motion toward the bed. "Can you stand up?" she asked.

Kelly got to her feet and fell forward at once. The nurse caught her and eased her into the bed.

"These infections are very dangerous," said the nurse. She had two pair of gloves on now. "Let me help you with those socks."

Overwhelmed with exhaustion, Kelly didn't even try to disagree.

"Why are you breathing so hard?" asked the nurse.

"I don't know, I just feel out of breath," answered Kelly.

"I need a blood sample," said the nurse.

The alcohol swab was ice cold against her skin, and she gasped with pain. She knew she had a fever, but she didn't know how bad it was until her skin was pierced by the needle and she felt the cold spreading through her leg. The needle was gone before she knew it.

Once the blanket was placed over her legs, the pain in her calf started to decrease. She started to smile as the nurse put an alligator clip on her finger. She thought that this had already happened, but she realized she had just been imagining things the first time. A monitor beeped, and she looked around for the source of the noise. Even turning her head was becoming painful. She touched her head with her hand, and the nurse noticed at once. She flicked a switch by the IV line, and the pain started to go away in seconds.

Kelly didn't notice how much time had passed before the doctor walked in. Everything around her was a fog.

The doctor turned on a bright light and pointed it at her eyes. The headache came back at once, pushing past the painkillers like they weren't flowing anymore. She put her hand over her eyes.

"Mm-hmm, light sensitivity. You've got Hantavirus, and it's progressing rapidly," said the doctor. "Mice around the world carry it. Your lungs are all inflamed, and you're not getting enough oxygen because of it. You're going to have to stay here until you're treated."

"But I do storytelling at the library every week," she said.

"That will have to wait until you get better," said the doctor.

"But I need to keep making money," she said.

"Not in your condition. I can't even remove the quarantine until the infection is gone."

Kelly tried to accept the idea that she couldn't leave, but then a consolation occurred to her. At least here the mouse couldn't bite her again. She would finally get some peace and quiet, a place all to herself. She just wanted that sanctuary without getting an infection at the same time. She wanted to get some time to write, but before the doctor left, the combination of her fever and the medicine in her body brought her to sleep.

Chapter Eighteen

The stiff muscles in her neck hadn't gone down by the second day in the hospital, but the nausea was becoming a problem. She needed IV fluids because she couldn't keep anything in her stomach. While she suffered, the medicine worked against the virus until it became a battle she could sense.

Kelly even got medicine to fight her fever, but the headache was the least of her worries. The fever brought strange images to her mind. Aside from the doctor who monitored her progress, no one else came into the quarantined room. She didn't even get any guests. As she sat in her isolated room, her mind rambled from idea to idea.

She felt a dog kissing her hand, and she looked down and noticed a beagle. The companionship made her feel calmer, and she enjoyed having someone there. It had brown spots all across its head, and the side of her bed was her favorite place to sleep. It would stare at her from time to time, but the presence of the dog was enough to keep her calm through the pain and the dizziness.

Kelly didn't know she was hallucinating until the nurse walked straight through the beagle. After the nurse left, the beagle came back to her side. The hallucination was quite intense. She could even feel the coldness of his wet nose and see the green glow of his eyes in the dim room.

When she noticed the phone by her bed, she lifted it up and dialed her own phone number.

"Hello?" said Virgil.

"Virgil! I'm in the hospital. That mouse bit me and I got really sick."

Virgil didn't say anything at all for a few seconds. "Sorry, what?" he asked. "I was watching TV. Let me turn it down real fast."

Did he even notice I was gone?

"That mouse bit me and now I'm in the hospital." She hoped that this would be enough to snap him out of it.

"Good, now I can use the car all I want," he answered. "We've been really busy over on those condos. I've been going over there every day."

Why is he worried about the car?

"Virgil, this is serious. This virus could have killed me. Don't you even care?"

Now that should work.

Virgil's answer was immediate. "Well, if it doesn't kill you, call me back when you get better, and I'll pick you up from the hospital. I've just been so busy lately. I promise you I'll be here when you get better."

Nope. Still doesn't care.

"I just think that you could care about me a little more," she said.

"Why? You're just a pain in the neck. That mouse hasn't hurt me at all, and I'm still reading to it."

"You haven't killed it yet?" she asked in disbelief.

"Nope."

"They can't release me if they know I could get bitten again. You really have to get rid of that mouse."

"Well, I guess you have to stay there then."

"I can't stay here forever," she answered. "Look, there's a doctor coming in now. He can explain it to you."

Kelly listened to the doctor's side of the conversation.

"Yes, Mr. Barrett, it's called Hantavirus and it comes from mice. The mouse is still alive? Mr. Barrett, you're not safe if the mouse is still alive. Have you been having any difficulty breathing? It could be life-threatening. Yes, she's recovering, but it will take a few weeks for her to get well enough to be released. Yes, you should come down here and get checked out to make sure you're all right. Well, no, I can't make you come down here, but I can't release her until you confirm that the mouse is dead. Because a cleaning crew has to remove the feces and the urine from the house. No, there are regulations about this kind of thing. I'll let you talk to the patient again."

Kelly took the phone with a sigh of relief. "So, Virgil, do

you understand what he's telling you?"

"Yes, I understand. I'll let Hector run around in the backyard, sweep the floors, and in a few weeks, you'll get better and come back home. And why did the doctor think I could do construction work if was having trouble breathing? I mean, the nerve of that man!"

She didn't expect Virgil to be quite so callous while she was in the hospital, but she knew that most men were quite focused on their work, while she had never done an honest day's work in her life. She had always wanted to, but writing had never provided a way for her to survive on her own.

"Well, I wish you wouldn't have torn up that contract," she answered. "We wouldn't have rodent problems and leaking ceilings if you'd let me sign it."

"Well, if I had kept playing football, we'd have pretty good money too, but handyman work doesn't pay as good as being on a football team. I could have been making millions of dollars a year. Sam Bradford just signed an eighteen-million-dollar contract, and that's just for one year. Just think about that for a moment next time!"

The line clicked, and she realized that he'd hung up on her. She put the phone back in the cradle, and then the weight of the humiliation bore down on her. She realized that Virgil had a right to be angry at her. After all, he didn't get sick and end up in the hospital, but she felt like she had a right to be angry too. It just seemed so unfair. She knew rationally that everyone had to make sacrifices, but it seemed like she was having to make a lot of sacrifices. His attitude cemented her desire to sign that contract and get away from Virgil. It wasn't so much a plan of getting somewhere else, just a basic urge to get away from him. The shortness of breath was made more tolerable by the oxygen, and she had been getting better sleep in the comfortable hospital bed. Her bed at home didn't have an elevated backrest, after all, or an oxygen mask.

The way Virgil had simply rejected her was almost too much for her to bear. It made her want to scream, but she knew that she was in no shape to scream out loud. She forced herself to calm down with sheer willpower and reminding herself that she could use a few weeks in bed, recovering from her illness, and being in a healthy environment.

Kelly got so angry she didn't want to call him back at all, but then she remembered that, as her husband, he was the only one who could legally pick her up from the hospital. Sarah was too far away, and her parents, even farther. The frustration just made her more upset, along with the illness, but the painkillers interfered with her feelings and soon her emotions subsided.

The days in the hospital seemed to take forever. With the lights turned down, it was hard to tell when it was day or night. The lights stayed on all night so the nurses could continue to observe her, and even though she protested, the doctor insisted that her condition was too fragile to neglect her overnight. She tried to object, but the breathing trouble made her dizzy. Once she had the oxygen mask on, she felt more relaxed, and she waited for the healing to take effect.

One surprise visitor came after she'd been in the hospital for about a month. Doug visited, and even though his voice was muffled by the mask, it still sounded just as sexy.

"Virgil told me you were sick, but the nurses filled me in a lot more."

Kelly took her oxygen mask off and smiled at him. "I'm not contagious anymore, am I?"

Doug shook his head. "Until they take away your breathing mask, you're not better yet."

Kelly heard the rattling in her lungs and put the oxygen mask back on before the coughing could start.

As she focused on breathing steadily, Kelly kept her eyes on Doug. He became a center to her, where she could feed off his calm energy to relax.

"Get well soon," he said before he walked away.

***

Five weeks after being admitted, Kelly had recovered enough to not need the oxygen mask, and the doctors said she was ready to go home. After a month and a half in a hospital bed, she felt prepared to leave the hospital, even if it meant that she'd have to go back to Virgil. She dreaded the return to the house where the mouse had undoubtedly continued to live. The hospital stay had been difficult, but she felt safe in the hospital bed with sanitizers nearby and no danger of a mouse running into her room.

In her own house, she didn't feel that same level of safety. She knew it was a bad thing to not feel safe in her own home, but she didn't have any idea where else she could live.

Kelly knew the mouse was still in her house, because she found tiny mouse droppings in the bathroom. She guessed that Virgil had neglected to sweep in there. The doctor's orders had not been enough motivation.

She grabbed a mousetrap from the top drawer by herself, set it down by the back door, and tried to load it with peanut butter. She had to keep the trap held open while she loaded it before getting the second mousetrap just to be safe. Then she delicately set the mousetraps up in the ceiling, because there was already a hole above the living room, and waited.

That evening, Virgil and Kelly were eating dinner. While they were working on their food, there was a loud snap, followed by a loud squeak. When Hector fell out of the ceiling, still attached to the mousetrap, and landed on Virgil's head, he almost lost his mind. He jumped up at once, knocking Hector aside, and the mouse hit the floor and stopped moving at once, weighed down by the mousetrap.

He held the mousetrap in front of her face. She pulled away in revulsion. "What are you doing? Get that ugly thing away from me!"

"Somebody killed Hector!" he said, crying. "I thought I got rid of all the mousetraps!"

Kelly gave him a dirty look. "I still can't believe you had the nerve to name that filthy animal. That mouse put me in the hospital. The doctor said that you were supposed to make it live outside. Do you want to catch the virus too? You'll be in the hospital for weeks, and then you won't be able to work at all."

Virgil went outside and dug a small hole in the front yard with a trowel while Kelly watched through the window in astonishment. Neil stared out his own window too. There he was, on his hands and knees, with tears going down his face as he gingerly pulled apart the trap. The mouse dropped into the hole. Virgil cried for another minute, wiping his face before wailing, "Here lies Hector, the best mouse I ever met."

Neil was staring through his window next door in wide-eyed horror. He hung his head, clearly unable to look at Virgil anymore. He looked at Kelly with deep sympathy, and slowly pulled the curtains shut.

Virgil came inside and tried to set his head in her lap, crying.

Kelly stood up and looked down at him. "Enough of this, Virgil! Can't you see you've changed? You're not going to lay a hand on me, or any food, or any chairs, or anything else until you wash your hands! I'm watching you!"

Virgil went to the sink without saying a word and washed his hands. She could tell that he felt remorse. He knew he was wrong. He was just too stubborn to admit it to her. She accepted his silence as evidence of his regret, but she knew that a real apology would be a long time coming.

Chapter Nineteen

It was several days later when Kelly opened the drawer under the sink looking for a saucepan to cook spaghetti sauce in. She found the big pan and lifted the lid, excited to get back to her home cooking. She couldn't find any saucepans at all, though, and she realized they were all catching leaks.

She went back inside, called up her debit card, and there was just enough for her to get a new saucepan and the gas money to get there. She knew that this would be too complicated for Virgil.

Sure, she would send him into town for a big pan, but he'd come back with a small pan and some beer. Or he would bring back a single coffee mug and a six-pack.

When she got home, she wanted to get started on the cooking, but she realized he was not alone. Doug was also there. As Kelly came inside, she noticed that Doug was looking at the broken frame above the door. She didn't even want him to see it, but she held her tongue so she could get a good look at his muscular back before he turned around. His T-shirt fit snugly enough that she could see every bulge.

"Hey, Kelly, Doug says he can get these things fixed around here!" Virgil was smiling.

"What? We can't afford this, Virgil. It cost the rest of our money just to get this new saucepan!"

Doug spoke up. "No, I want to do it for free this weekend! It would free up some of your other saucepans once all the leaks are gone."

"Now hang on just a second, I'm not too sure about this," Kelly said. "Why would you want to do this for free? What's in it for you?"

Virgil turned to Kelly, glaring vividly. "Come on, Kelly,

don't be like that. This guy is being nice enough to offer to work on the house."

Doug nodded. "Exactly. I don't mind doing it for free. Helping you two out is the least I can do. Virgil's been very helpful at work." Kelly looked at Virgil in surprise. "So you don't mind if I get rid of all those dripping sounds you have to hear all day?"

Kelly looked at Doug gratefully. "Thank you for your kindness, but it's just hard to believe anyone would do anything at all for free these days."

Doug answered, "Not a problem at all. I'd better get going, though. I've got to pick up some tar paper and some fresh tar for the roof before I get home."

After Doug left, Virgil said, "Kelly, I need to talk to you."

Now Kelly knew she finally had a chance to confront him. "I need to talk to you too. Why is the bank account so short on cash? Did you buy more beer?"

Virgil was offended. "No, of course not! I had to buy some tools for work."

"Well, he'd better keep paying you because we need more money. I appreciate getting the house fixed up, but what we really need is money. How come you're working so hard now? You never put any effort in around here." Kelly knew she sounded desperate, but she didn't care. When Virgil got her this mad, she always got more defensive, because when push came to shove, Virgil was able to shove pretty hard.

"I'm picking up the check on Friday, and every Friday after this." said Virgil, crossing his arms. "What about you? Have you made any money off your stories yet?"

Kelly felt a flood of anger when Virgil started rubbing it in. "Just the library money. I had a chance, Virgil, and you took it away from me. Why?"

As usual, Virgil tried to tear her down again. "I was trying to protect you. You know that! They would have kept eighty percent of all the profits! That's just not right! Why should they get rich when you're the one who wrote the story? Don't fall for these sharks. Why do you keep this silly dream? Why do you keep all those rejection letters if it makes you so depressed?"

"It doesn't make me depressed. It motivates me. But

then you tell me the contract's no good and I don't know what to think! I have to accept something, don't I? Even if it's only twenty percent of the profits, at least it's something in the bank!"

"Kelly, you've never made a lick of sense to me," said Virgil.

Kelly lost her temper. "Well, you never understood me at all, even the day you met me. I don't know why you still want to be with me if you don't understand me! I'm going to take a walk!"

As she was leaving, Virgil yelled, "Hey! What about my dinner?"

"Make dinner for yourself, I'm not hungry!" she shot back and closed the door.

Kelly headed down the driveway, hoping that a good walk would change her mood.

However, she had barely begun out her front door when she saw Neil staring at her again, chuckling this time too. He was standing in his living room, but his curtains were wide open and he was staring at her. She flipped him off as she kept walking, and he closed the curtains very quickly.

The colors of sunset shone overhead, the yellow-tinged clouds making her feel calm and peaceful. In the cool twilight, she felt her tension leaving as her muscles pushed forward, felt them unlocking and unwinding as she kept striding, stretching her legs to get rid of the strain. The flowering purple sage cleared her mind with its dense aroma.

She had barely made it down the road a few hundred feet before she heard the Blazer driving slowly behind her. Since its drive up the hill, the engine had been coughing. She knew it was Virgil. A few more seconds and he'd be driving right next to her, bothering her again.

Yep, there he is, she thought as he drove up.

"Come on, honey. I get paid on Friday. I'll put the money back."

"You just don't get it, do you?" Kelly said.

"Get what? Get in the Blazer, honey!" Virgil was getting impatient.

"It's no use, you just don't get it!"

Kelly got into the vehicle, but made sure the door slammed.

Virgil breathed in slowly, and then breathed out even slower. Kelly knew that he was aware of how much she hated that.

As he turned around, headed back for home, she felt all the doubts creeping in. What if she wasn't good enough? What if she was wasting her time trying to find an agent? Virgil was always making her feel insecure.

For the rest of the night, Virgil maintained an uneasy silence while Kelly got ready for bed and fell asleep. Grateful for the break from his complaining, Kelly fell asleep quickly and didn't wake up until Virgil got up for work. He muttered, "Have fun with Doug today" as he headed out of the bedroom.

Chapter Twenty

Kelly heard Virgil leaving the house in the tired Blazer early in the morning. The sun hadn't even come up yet. She looked at the alarm clock. It read 6:30. She wanted to go back to sleep, but her body refused, and the more she thought about Doug, the more impossible it became, so she got out of bed.

She got dressed carefully, but she still thought the clothes in her closet made her look cheap. She started the coffeepot, still feeling uneasy about Virgil's absence, and eating a bowl of cereal as she waited for the coffee. Even if he was showing up for work on time, it seemed like he was really jealous of Doug as well.

As she drank her coffee, she worked on her second bowl of cereal.

Whenever he was really jealous, Virgil would leave early in the morning, come home late, not talk to her, and basically act like she wasn't even there. She knew that it was his way of getting even with her. Even as a child, he had never lacked for attention, and he knew that if he stayed quiet long enough, she'd break down and pay attention to him again.

She could tell it was going to be a hot day today. The sky was free of clouds, and the morning shadows were deep and heavy, but the road was already beginning to show heat waves blurring the houses beyond.

The smell of rotten eggs beneath the sink was getting unbearable, and she knew the heat was making the mold grow like crazy because of the awful stench. It got so bad that she put her cereal bowl in the sink. She turned on the tap, but then she had to wait for the water to come out.

While she was drinking more coffee and waiting for enough water to rinse the bowl, she heard a truck pull up in

Virgil's spot. It was Doug's work truck. CARLTON CONSTRUCTION, it said on the side, in red letters that re- minded her of Legos. Pipes and boards were sticking out of the bed of the truck, even though she could tell it was one of the big ones, at least a sixteen-foot. Virgil would have been able to tell her which model it was. He was crazy about big trucks, especially if they had the seven-foot high tires under them.

The only person to get out of the truck was Doug. She felt her hands getting sweaty and she put her coffee cup down so she wouldn't drop it. She went outside to meet him. Even though they were alone, her hands started to get shaky with nervousness. "You're alone? Where are your helpers?"

"Oh," he said, laughing, "I'm just here to fix the sink. I don't know what Virgil told you about it, but it's a one-man job. You can't fit anybody else under there when I'm working on it. In fact, you can just keep doing what you want. I've got this covered."

Kelly started to get very excited, but the sink had beaten her and Virgil time and again, so she felt a sense of relief that someone professional was finally working on it.

"Well, I'm glad you know what you're doing. Every time Virgil gets under there, it just gets worse. That dripping is driving me crazy, and sometimes it doesn't even want to drain at all and I have to pour Drano down it. But it doesn't matter, because even when it's clogged, it still leaks from under the sink basin, too, so the water eventually goes away."

Doug nodded his head. "But the water is also ruining the cabinet under the sink," he said. "I can smell the mold. I'm going to have to clean that up too. This might take a while."

"Sorry about the smell," Kelly said.

"Don't apologize, please. That's what I'm here for." Opening his workbox, he pulled out two breathing masks. "Here you go," he said, handing her one. He touched her hand when she took the mask and it made tingles go down her spine.

Kelly could tell this guy was different than the other handymen she'd met. He was more professional.

"You have a pump house somewhere or a town water line?"

"It's our own water," she said. "It's over there, down past the lilacs." She led him around the bushes until he found the green box where Virgil had the main valve.

"This is the only valve?"

"No, there's one up by the spring, too."

Doug started to laugh again. "Well, if we don't shut that one off, it'll just make this pipe break."

Kelly wondered if this had been to blame for Virgil's plumbing disasters. It seemed more than clear to her at once, and the flash of rage at his ignorance didn't go away. "Ignorance is not bliss," she said out loud, and Doug nodded.

He set to work getting the water shut off with a long yellow tool that looked like a weed ripper she'd use in her garden, but even longer.

"That looks awesome. Last time Virgil had to do that, he was on his belly with his arm stuck down that shaft for ten minutes, trying to do it by hand."

"Well, it's too bad he hadn't met me back then. I could have shown him this valve wrench. Does Virgil ever do any work around here at all?"

"Hardly anything."

Kelly liked watching construction people when they knew what they were doing. She noticed Neil staring at her then and was relieved when Doug went inside and she could get away from her creepy neighbor.

Doug took a look under the sink. "Well, this inlet for the dishwasher is backward, so that's half of the problem right there."

"That dishwasher never worked at all."

Doug crawled back out from under the sink and looked at her in a puzzled way. "Virgil never noticed that the dishwasher wasn't getting any water?"

"Oh, he noticed, but he never could figure out how to fix it."

Doug started to laugh. "Well, the incoming water line runs to the outgoing pipe, and the outflow water goes straight to the inlet. This isn't an easy fix, but it's better than sending water back down to the pump."

"Aren't I getting in your way? I should get some writing done," she said.

Kelly went inside. She remembered the dog Houdini that

she used to have. She could imagine Houdini scooching underneath a wooden fence. Soon, she had Houdini in the story, and the fence. She only got a little writing done before Doug started banging around underneath the sink. She thought she would be able to handle it, but as the banging continued, she realized she wasn't going to get anything accomplished.

Whatever was wrong, it must have been pretty stuck, because Doug was starting to talk to the sink, urging it to break loose. It was impossible for her to concentrate with a man working in her kitchen. She stood up and went into the kitchen where more interesting things were happening.

The banging had been replaced by a lot of squeaking, which was even more annoying. She found herself staring at those legs of his sticking out of his cargo shorts under her sink, and the sound became less distracting. Unlike Virgil's legs, they seemed to have no hair at all, just some light peach fuzz.

Way more interesting than writing.

The stench was gone from the kitchen, and that alone brought a smile to her face. His legs kept her smiling, and her writing tasks were entirely forgotten.

I can't put sexy legs in a children's book. Maybe I need to do more adult writing.

The squeaking stopped, and then she heard a splash. Quickly, his legs started moving and Doug came out from under the sink. "Got it!" he said, holding up a piece of pipe. It was full of sludge. "That's what's wrong with your sink. The trap was upside down, and the inlet was clogged too, but I should have no problem getting this in good working order. I'll have them replaced in no time!"

Kelly was overjoyed, and a tension that had tugged at her shoulders for years budged at last.

"Thank you, I'm so happy. That dripping was making it so hard to focus."

"These inflow hoses were leaking too, so I'm just going to replace them at the same time, okay?" Doug was starting up with the squeaking again, trying to loosen another hose, which was probably as white and crusted with sediment as the pipe he had recently kicked out.

Doug got up off the floor and dropped the filthy old pipes

into the garbage can. Then he went outside and came in a few minutes later with a bunch of copper pipes.

"Wow!" she said. "These look much nicer than those black plastic pipes any day. Now it's not going to be so scary-looking under my sink."

"Plastic pipes don't even belong under your sink, just copper ones."

Kelly went back to writing, but the air was getting hotter inside the house. She went to the air conditioner and turned it on, but it didn't help very much. It seemed to be on its last legs with the motor banging and clattering. It was so hot she had to wipe the sweat off her forehead so it wouldn't get into her eyes.

Doug went back outside and took off his shirt because of the heat. Kelly watched him from the window as he went around his truck, digging through the back for more plumbing supplies. "Oh, good, something else to watch."

Kelly tried to concentrate on the writing, but the heat kept rising and the air conditioner struggled to compensate. She got several lines done before Doug went outside again. When she could see him in the front yard with the valve turner, she wrote nothing at all because her attention was fixed on him.

After Doug had been working for a while, she couldn't help herself and went back to the kitchen. There was more squeaking under the sink, and Doug's leg was tapping in rhythm.

"It's lunchtime," she said, and Doug's leg stopped. "I don't have anything but bologna, sorry."

Doug came out from under the sink. "I brought my own sandwich. I just got the sink fixed up. I got your water line back on. Let me just run the tap for a few seconds and we should be back in water." He turned on the tap for cold water as high as he could. Loud bangs and groans echoed through the pipe.

"Is it supposed to do that?"

"Just listen, that's the sound of fresh water coming your way."

The bangs became thumps and the groaning turned into a roar as ice-cold water started pouring out of the faucet. A couple seconds after the water started gushing, it stopped flowing completely, coughed, and suddenly resumed the volley of water. Kelly stared at the sink for a good half-minute, surprised that the water wasn't backing up into the sink at all anymore but sucking down the drain in a smooth whirlpool.

As she looked at the cold water pouring out of her sink, Kelly realized she was getting way too hot and she needed to cool down. She undid her ponytail so it wouldn't stop the water from hitting her scalp.

"What are you doing?" asked Doug. "I told you it was going to work."

She had expected at least a wolf whistle when she undid her ponytail, but Doug surprised her by not mentioning it.

"That sink used to be really slow. Now I can get myself cooled off," she answered. "I've been waiting for this all morning, because it keeps getting hotter and hotter."

Kelly knew that other women would use water to make themselves more attractive, since it made their nipples stand out. All she wanted to do was cool off, though.

She stuck her head under the faucet. Even though she was very hot and could feel the heat radiating off her neck, the water surprised her with its chilling grasp. For a moment, her throat constricted, and breathing was painful, and then the spasm left her neck and she indulged in the cooling water.

"Oh wow, this is a lifesaver," she said.

It was much colder than it had been before the sink was fixed, and she suspected that was also Virgil's fault, because now with the new pipes, the water flowed fast and icy. She pulled her head out from under the faucet and backed away from the sink, letting the droplets fall down her shirt and cool her body off.

Doug was looking at her with a grin on his face. Kelly didn't realize that men could still look at her that way. It gave her a thrill to know that she was still attractive.

"I was just going to get a drink of water myself, but that looks so nice. Do you mind?"

Kelly looked at Doug in surprise, not expecting him to be so courteous, a quality Virgil despised and usually rebelled against. "Go right ahead," she said, glad for the change of attitude.

Doug quickly submerged himself under the running fau-

cet, covering his head and neck in cold water. She noticed
how dark tan the back of his neck was and felt pity for him.
Even though Virgil had been a steady worker for Doug, he
never came home with a sunburn, and Doug's skin was per-
manently darkened.

After getting himself soaked in the sink, grabbing a glass
from the cabinet, and filling it with water, Doug sat down at
the table. "That's much better!" he said before he drank a
generous amount. He set the glass back down on the table
and stared ahead, breathing deeply and stretching his back
now that the job was done.

"How did you get into construction in the first place?"
Kelly asked. Since Virgil was still gone, she didn't mind having some conversation.

"My father was in the construction business. He made all
sorts of money back in the day. I worked for him and he
taught me the skills. I guess I'm just carrying on the family
business."

"Oh, you're a rich kid." She scowled. *How is he going to
understand me? He doesn't know anything about struggling.*

"You don't care for rich people?" he asked.

It's about my struggles, not that he's rich. "You have
money, you wouldn't understand."

Doug looked offended by this comment, and Kelly regret-
ted it immediately. "That's what you think?" he asked. "You
think I'm rich? Contractors only make twenty dollars an hour.
I live in a totally normal apartment. It's my father that's living the high life. He got to build some of those hotels over on
the ocean. When you're working on a single project for
years, the money starts to pile up pretty fast. After a couple
weeks, I'm looking for work again."

Kelly avoided looking at her own house, but it still made
her feel inferior to even imagine the fancy hotels. "I just
don't want you looking at me any differently because I'm not
rich. It's like rich people think poverty is contagious or something. When people find out I'm poor, they just don't look at
me the same."

Doug raised his hand, and Kelly stopped talking. It was
refreshing to have a polite man in the house. Virgil would
have just started talking right over her.

"You're just being negative, Kelly. You need to change

your perception."

Kelly didn't want to change her mood, but it was impossible because she knew he was right.

"The way Virgil acts at work, I can see why he keeps going from job to job. He doesn't love what he's doing. He's just doing it to get paid, and he doesn't do it very well."

That doesn't take a lot of perception, but at least he's noticing me. She noticed the negative thought turn into a positive one and she felt better at once.

"When I work on people's houses, it's because I love helping people in need. I see broken things and I want to fix them. That's just the way I am. If there's something dripping in my apartment, I'm the same way. I just get in there and fix it. For me, it's always been about being able to help others. By the time I'm fifty, I'll be too old to do construction, and then I can relax and retire, but I'll never lose that passion for helping other people."

Kelly changed the subject because charity still made her uncomfortable, even if he had his reasons. She wanted to focus on something else besides her broken down house. "Do you have any kids? Anyone as nice as you should have at least one kid to spoil rotten."

"Yes, I do; they're the joys of my life. One is six and one is eight. Their mother was a cheerleader in high school. By the time I realized what I was getting into, it was too late. I took her over for dinner, and my father noticed that she was pregnant. He took me out back so she couldn't hear him and told me in no uncertain terms that I had to do the right thing by her. So, we got married. I had no choice."

Kelly tried to stay positive, but the children Doug mentioned hit a raw nerve. It was one difference between them that she'd never be able to repair. "Children would be liberating for me. I don't have any kids of my own, and, according to the doctor, I'll never have any in the future either. That's why it makes me so happy to go to the library and read to the children."

"Well, look on the bright side, at least you're doing that," Doug said. "You're so great with kids. Nobody else wants your job anyway. I never even saw any 'story time' at the library until you started reading there."

Kelly knew she needed to be more positive, but it was

just so difficult with Virgil always being mean to her. She wasn't used to positive reactions. Virgil had always been critical of her library work.

"By the way, Virgil's been complaining about his missing red wrench for the last two days. Do you know what happened to it?"

"He dropped it on the driveway almost a week ago," said Kelly. "I meant to give it back to him, but he's always arguing with me so I forget. It's back there by the bathroom. I'm surprised he didn't see it this morning. If he ever decides to work on the bathroom, he'll notice it. Now I just wish my roof would stop leaking."

"So there are leaks in the living room and the bathroom too?" Doug asked. Kelly showed Doug to the living room and he stood for a few seconds just staring at the wall of rejection letters. "So, why do you keep all those rejection letters? It's a fire hazard," he asked.

Kelly answered, "When I look at them, it gives me inspiration. I know it sounds a little silly, but it motivates me. I look at them and I keep thinking about the day when one of those letters is going to say: 'we have accepted your story.'"

"I hate to tell you, but this could catch fire, you know?" Doug looked around the house at the pans. "It leaks in all these different places?" He looked at the ceiling, then went back into the kitchen too. When he came back, he said, "I'm glad I brought plenty of tar paper. It looks like you're going to end up replacing this whole side of the roof. But as far as your sink, it won't drip anymore, at least not for another thirty years or so."

Kelly wiped her brow with her hand because she was getting sweaty. She went outside, and the breeze was an instant relief. A large cloud drifted through the sky, and the shade brought even more comfort. Doug went to his truck and got the ladder. Kelly enjoyed watching him climb up. When he started removing the shingles, it looked like he didn't even have to pull. They flew through the air one by one.

"I'll pick them up when I'm done," said Doug. Kelly stayed far away from the pile of sun-bleached shingles. She kept stealing glances at Doug as he worked. "This tar is so thin I can put my finger through it," he complained.

She knew she was looking at Doug a lot, but she couldn't help it. His legs, his arms, everything had muscles. Sure, he was complaining about the state of the roof, but he was doing something about it.

Kelly went to the garden hose and sprayed the water straight up into the air. A torrent of splashes cooled her body in the summer heat.

"That looks like fun!" said Doug from where he was standing on the roof.

Kelly didn't mind the attention. She called up to him, "Well, I'd be happy to spray you down too. You look pretty hot up there!"

Doug got down off the ladder and grabbed another hose. He sent a fountain of water up into the air, and as it splashed down all over him, Kelly noticed the gooseflesh rising on his skin. Doug kept moving the hose back and forth to stay under the waterfall.

Kelly started giggling wildly and sprayed Doug with her hose too, knocking him off balance. He regained his footing quickly and looked back up at her, also chuckling. He pointed his hose at her and started soaking her. Spraying one another, they ran towards each other, getting soaking wet.

She was too caught up in the moment to pay attention to Neil, who was no doubt staring at them in intense fascination.

The grass was getting slippery from all the water, and they sort of slid into each other's arms, bumping into an awkward embrace, hands flying everywhere as they struggled for balance. Then they stopped sliding, held each other, and stared, not knowing what to say.

Doug was the first one to break the silence. Embarrassed, he walked back a step, and said, "Well, I'd better get finished on the roof. I've got lots of good sunlight and it looks like I should be able to get the new tarpaper down by sunset. Did you know you need a whole inch of tar to keep the rain out? You really bought quite a fixer-upper."

"It really wasn't so bad when we bought it."

Doug chuckled, but climbed the ladder again.

Chapter Twenty-One

After he got done working on the roof, Doug went home, exhausted. He hadn't been doing as much roofing as he had before he earned the rank of contractor, and the hard work on the baking surface had him worn out.

"Where have you been?" said Danielle, his wife. "The kids miss you! They get more time with their grandfather than with you. That's where they are today! I can't just make them stay here all day!"

Danielle had shoulder-length dishwater hair and blue eyes. After the kids, she was 140 pounds, but she was five-and-a-half feet. Her nose was kind of pointed at the end, and it always made her look sterner. Tonight, her whole body looked stern. She was even pointing her finger at him.

"That's not fair. You know I spend as much time with my kids as I can. I've been fixing this guy's house that works for me."

"But all that time you're helping other people, you could be at home raising your kids." Danielle's disappointment had turned to resentment, and now she was fuming. But Doug was getting tired of her attitude.

This wasn't the first time she had mentioned all the time she spent taking care of the kids. When the kids were in their diaper phases, she was always making him change them. Back then, he'd end up getting to the job site half an hour late sometimes.

"You know I like helping people. I wish you'd quit throwing that back in my face. You should be grateful you have a roof that doesn't leak. Lots of people just slap a little tar on their roof and call it good. They don't know what they're doing. This one guy's roof, it was just about to collapse it was built so badly. I'm sure you don't want our children in some dripping, leaking building, do you? The kids would be getting sick all the time!"

"You always have to play the hero, don't you?" She scowled, but her shoulders went up, and he knew he'd won that round.

"Once the kids get back from my dad's I'll take them to Splash Montana for the day. Is that fair enough?"

"Oh, I see. So you just don't want to spend any time with me. Is that it?"

"I don't have time to argue with you. I've got stuff to do in the garage."

"Fine then!" said Danielle. "You're always busy, aren't you?"

Doug decided not to answer her this time and just headed off down the hill toward the garage, where all his construction ideas took shape. He knew that there would be consequences for ignoring her, but he really didn't care anymore. The passion had faded away, and it was just the matter of having two kids that kept him from walking away entirely. He couldn't imagine those kids without a roof over their heads, and he knew Danielle had no way of making money by herself with the kids to take care of.

Tonight, he was planning on building an organizer for Kelly. He found a nice sheet of metal with shells embossed into it, and he polished it up, removing the rust. When it was done, all he would have to do was give her some magnets and she would have a nice fireproof wall for anything she wanted.

Doug kept himself busy polishing the metal for a while, but before he could get it done, his buddy George came over with a few beers. Once Doug saw the beers, he realized how overheated he still was, so he sat down with George and they drank together for a while.

George focused on the beers while Doug drank his and stared at the sheet he was in the middle of polishing. "Hey, buddy, you're pretty quiet today."

"I've just been thinking a lot lately. You know Virgil's wife?"

"Yeah. She is quite a looker." George was prone to wandering eyes when he drank. He'd already called dozens of women "lookers" when Doug was around.

"I was working on her house today and she was getting herself wet to cool off. I got myself cooled off too. But I kind of slipped into her, and we both stood there for a few seconds. It was really strange, like we had a connection, like we were meant to run into each other."

"Hey, man, don't be getting big ideas like that into your poor head. My wife would literally kill me if I even thought about hooking up. Once, I was staring at this girl in a restaurant, and I only got in about three seconds of looking before my wife stuck her fork into my hand. It took the doctors an hour to sew my palm back up."

George's pocket phone went off, with its annoying "William Tell Overture" ringtone he'd reserved for when his wife called him. "Oh, man, that's the cavalry right now. I've got to get going. See you later. Hey, keep the last beer. I don't want my wife seeing it."

Doug grabbed the last beer and cracked it, taking a swing, and then said, "See you around, George. Watch your back."

He worked on the door for a few hours, playing back the image in his mind of the two of them on the lawn over and over until it flared bright. He couldn't get the moment out of his head, and he wanted to feel her skin at least once more. Then he looked at the clock and realized it was getting late. He went to bed. His wife slept in her own room, so she didn't care when he got up or went to bed. She was already asleep. All the lights in the house were off. The kids had stayed at his dad's house again because his dad was rich and had a fancy pool. The pool and the money made the kids love his dad more than him.

Doug was happy with the way things were, though, and reminded himself not to complain as he went to bed all by himself, leaving his clothes next to the bed since Danielle hardly ever bothered to come into his room anymore, and even if she did, Doug knew she would be more interested in yelling at him about something else instead of where he dropped his dirty clothes.

Chapter Twenty-Two

Doug came over again the next morning to finish the roof. Kelly watched him lay out rolls of fresh roofing paper. When he was done, though, he only went to his truck for a moment.

"I've got a surprise for you."

"For me?" Kelly tried to hide her enthusiasm, but she clapped her hands.

Doug pulled a sheet of metal out of the pickup. "It's for organizing your writing ideas. Most writers have boards like this. I've got all these magnets I've been collecting from old VCRs. They're perfect for this kind of thing."

Kelly looked deep into his sky-blue eyes. "Thank you so much. It's been a long time since anybody's done something nice for me."

Doug brought the magnet board inside. After hanging it up on the wall, he went back to the truck and gave her a pack of index cards with magnets on the back. "Now you can build your stories on this board before you even start writing them down."

"It's perfect! Thank you so much! Plus, it will give me something else to look at besides those rejection letters."

Doug said, "Exactly! That's why you're welcome. The pleasure's all mine. Well, I'd better get going, I have to get back to my job. But my kids can't wait to see you on Wednesday for story time."

On Wednesday afternoon, Doug pulled up at the library with his kids, both boys dressed in blue T-shirts, and merged with other children.

Kelly began. "Today, I'm going to tell you a story called *The Fox and the Crow*. Once upon a time, there were three lumberjacks who lived with their father in the deep woods."

As she continued her story, Doug found himself captivated by her, the way her luscious red lips were moving, and the way they nudged slightly to the left whenever she smiled so it was almost a half-smile. He also noticed the way she hid her teeth with her lips as if she was self-conscious.

Kelly read from her story, "As the fox ate the berries, he didn't feel so good, but the crow laughed at him and insisted that he keep eating. The fox knew he couldn't eat any more berries, but he still wanted the wood from the crow's tree."

Again, Doug got lost in her voice, and he stared at her as she acted out the fox with her hands squeezed in front of her, and all the children laughed. Before he knew it, the story was over, and all the children were clapping and laughing.

Doug watched a mother come over to Kelly and ask her, "Is there anywhere I can find your wonderful stories?"

Doug heard Kelly answer, "Not yet, but I'm not giving up hope."

Doug was surprised that Kelly had never gotten any books published. He remembered some literary agents that he'd met over the years, and resolved to look up their addresses when he got home.

Chapter Twenty-Three

After she got done with story time, Tammy kept looking at her, and she got the hint pretty quick that they needed to talk in some privacy. They ended up in a quiet park.

"That guy was really staring at you a lot, Kelly, the one in the shorts. You two have some real chemistry. I hope you know his name."

Kelly laughed, waving the suggestion away. "Oh, of course I know his name, that's just Doug. He's doing some work on my house."

Kelly was glad for the privacy. She knew that her face was getting red just thinking about him.

Tammy couldn't keep the smirk off her face. "When a guy stares at you like that, Kelly, he's into you."

"But I'm married to Virgil! You know that, no matter what he does, I'm never going to cheat on him."

"When was the last time you went out anywhere? You know what you really need? You need some time away from that house. I've got a barn dance this Friday. You need to go down there and shake your sillies out."

"It's been months since I went out. But I have to tell Virgil first. He's not going to like it."

"Screw Virgil! You know how much I hate the way he treats you. Go anyway!"

When Kelly got home, she found Virgil in the living room. As she suspected, he was watching TV and eating food at the same time. Some of it was getting on the couch; lettuce leaves from the burger adorned the cushions like confetti. Of course, at the end of the day, she always had to clean it up. That's how it always went.

"Hey, Virgil, I've got a question. Tammy's got a barn dance on Friday."

Virgil put the paper wrapper down on the sofa. The burger dropped more lettuce leaves. "But there's a show on Syfy Friday night I was going to watch."

"Be that way then, but I'm going! How come you never use a plate?"

"The paper holds the burger together or else they wouldn't put it on there!"

"You're impossible!" Kelly shouted. "Sometimes I wish I'd never married you!"

Kelly went to bed early, trying to avoid Virgil, but when he came to bed, he was eager as ever. She let him do what he wanted to her, but she felt disgusted by it.

Chapter Twenty-Four

Kelly got dressed in her bright red dress and headed out to the car, feeling relief when Virgil stared ineffectively at his TV show and didn't even notice she wore her best clothing as she went out.

Closing the door, Kelly felt a sense of finality. It was just a barn dance, but the feeling of separation was unavoidable. She considered leaving him for good, but she knew that he would probably keep watching TV even if she did take off.

She put Virgil out of her mind and focused on the night ahead. She was able to look forward to at least four hours without Virgil trying to tear down her self-esteem, and she didn't want to waste any of that time thinking about him.

The barn dance was in full swing by the time Kelly arrived. Before she got there, she was already thinking about Doug, so it didn't surprise her that his truck was parked in the driveway among all the other trucks and cars. She counted fifty cars before she realized that she couldn't count them all. It was going to be a real party.

The band was playing up-tempo bluegrass music. It was very loud, but Kelly thought bluegrass should be that way. She enjoyed good-time music like this. She was surprised to see Doug's wife, a woman with blonde hair, talking with Doug in the gravel amongst the cars. She started to feel awkward. Cold night air made her shiver.

Tammy noticed her and came over, and Kelly felt a little safer, having someone she could trust at the barn dance.

"Did you know Doug was going to be here?" Kelly asked.

"Oh, yes, he brought his wife. Oh, there he is."

Kelly tried to look the other way, but Doug noticed her and called out, "Hey, Kelly!" His wife started walking over too. Feeling even more awkward now, she looked at the sky for support from above. She saw stars and cold pale clouds, but she still had to meet Doug's wife, because she was still walking over.

"Hey, Kelly, this is Danielle. Danielle, this is Kelly, the woman who needed some work on her house."

"Oh, so you're my husband's latest charity case," Danielle said. "Doug always has people that he takes care of." She stopped talking, blinked, looked off to the side, distracted, and veered off across the lawn without even saying goodbye, just shouting the names of her friends. "Annabelle! Bridget!"

Kelly was still trying to process the insult and also trying to hide her reaction to Danielle's statement, but since Danielle had already left, she didn't see any reason to keep smiling, even though Doug was chuckling.

Doug looked at her departing figure for a few seconds, but then turned his attention back to Kelly, bursting into full-blown laughter as the crowd clapped and hooted inside.

"What's so funny?"

"Oh, she's just going to spend time with her friends now. She does this every time. When the band stops making music, she'll hunt me down again."

The singer in the band had finished talking to the audience, and the music picked up again, another fast bluegrass dance.

"Would you like to dance?" asked Doug.

"What about your wife? Shouldn't you be dancing with her?" Kelly said.

"Oh, don't mind her insults. She'll be talking to Annabelle and Bridget all night. She only comes to these dances to ignore me and waste time with her rude friends."

Doug led her inside the barn, where the music pounded, and it must have been something about the golden light in the barn or the way Doug's hand felt so strong as he led her to the dance floor, but she found herself caught up in the moment. She was ready when Doug put his other hand on her waist and they started dancing. Kelly felt her pulse speed up until her ears were throbbing in time with the music.

The music was getting so loud it was hard to hear Doug. Kelly felt overwhelmed by the sound. She was about to tell him how she was feeling when Doug leaned in for a kiss at the end of the song. The dancers exploded with cheering and applause, and the noise and the unexpected kiss were all too much for her.

Kelly detached herself from Doug and backed out of the barn. She turned around and walked away from the noise. With all the people around, she had no idea where Danielle was, but she was hoping to stay away from her. The crush of people surrounded her and made her feel claustrophobic, but eventually, each one of them cleared out of the way and she could get free. She felt like she was running out of air. It turned into a strong feeling of asthma. She coughed and tried to take deep breaths as she kept coughing to force the air through her lungs.

From the press of bodies in the overcrowded barn to the shock of cool air on her skin, Kelly felt a huge shift of energy. Swept away from the crowd, she felt like she could breathe again. Without the trigger, she could process the panic attack she just had and start to calm down.

Even in the quiet, the throbbing in her ears wouldn't go away, and as she walked among the cars and trucks, she heard footsteps behind her.

"Kelly, wait! I know you're panicking."

Kelly realized she had to stop walking. Her lungs wouldn't let her continue. She leaned against a nearby Buick for support, far away from her own parking spot. This allowed him to catch up as her ears continued to pound, but with less intensity as she started to relax. She appreciated the gentle touch on her shoulder.

"As long as that music plays, Danielle dances. I told you not to worry about her."

"That's not it," she said, lying. "It was just too many people."

Doug wasn't even breathing heavy after all the dancing. "I told you, she doesn't waste a moment thinking about you. Kelly, I can't stop thinking about you. I've got to talk to you."

"Why? I'm married."

Doug answered at once, spoiling her angle. "So am I, but Kelly, those stories you write are amazing."

"Is that why you are out here talking to me?"

"I know some people in that business I might be able to talk to. Agents, managers, promoters."

"How am I supposed to believe that? I bet you don't

know a single agent!"

"Actually, I know five. I'm just trying to help you. And I wanted to apologize for Danielle too."

"Don't bother. I don't want to be your charity case!" She was about to say more, but Doug interrupted her.

"Don't even think about calling yourself that! Those are her words, not mine! Everybody I've ever helped has suffered her wrath. I don't think she wants anybody to be happy." He gave her a card after she finally got back in the Blazer. "Hey, if you ever decide you want to talk to me again, here's my number."

Kelly took his card, and she wrote down her number on a piece of paper. "Here's my number, Doug. But you'd better start connecting me to those agents. I've had a lifetime of rejection with Virgil, and I don't need another laundry list of broken promises. Do you know what he did the other day? He tore up a publishing contract."

As she looked at him, he answered, "You look really beautiful tonight." The comment caught her off guard, because she wasn't expecting it. It came out of nowhere and it broke through her defenses. She leaned forward, vulnerable and expecting romance, and he moved in for a kiss. As their lips were about to meet, Danielle's shrill voice burst out of the barn. "Hey, Doug! I want to get home now! My feet are killing me!"

Doug turned away to leave after squeezing her hands for a moment. With the romantic instance come and passed, staying at the dance was pointless.

Kelly drove the Blazer back to the highway, returning home to the same life that she left behind for a few sweet hours. Virgil still didn't look at her when she came home. She looked at the TV to see what was keeping his attention, and the Syfy channel he was watching advertised a marathon of *Quantum Leap*. She knew he would be up all night. Sure enough, when she woke up in the morning, Virgil was snoring next to her, so she knew that he had come to bed and had fallen asleep at once.

Chapter Twenty-Five

Kelly got a text on her phone the next afternoon.

I wanted so bad to kiss you last night. If you felt the same way, meet me for coffee at Bozeman Blends.

Kelly put the phone down and leaned back. She did feel the same way. She had been wondering what kissing Doug again would feel like. At the same time, she also felt conflicted because she hadn't made that choice before. No one else had ever gotten her to feel like she wanted to betray Virgil. She wondered if it was just because Virgil had been unusually grumpy for the last few weeks, but the more she thought about Doug's strong body wrapped around hers in the front yard, the more she realized that she really did want him.

Before she got ready, she headed out to the backyard. She uncovered the lunchbox holding scraps of paper and opened it to make sure the scraps were still inside. Despite being concealed by a thin layer of dirt, the lunchbox had stayed away from Virgil's attention.

Kelly knew she couldn't take the chance that he would find it.

She got dressed in a red shirt and blue jeans and headed out of the bedroom. She went back into the living room, where Virgil was still watching TV, and she lied. "Tammy and I are going out to dinner. See you later."

Virgil said, "Mm-hmm," and never took his eyes off the TV. It made her feel better that he was continuing to ignore her, like whatever she did wasn't important to him.

Maybe he won't even mind if I tell him what I'm doing.

Kelly tried to ignore her neighbor as she headed to the car, but the long wolf whistle from next door reminded her that Neil was still watching. She flipped him off as she walked to the Blazer, wishing he would leave her alone. Neil wasn't the person she wanted to get that kind of attention from. Doug had far more manners and treated her like he actually cared about her.

Twice she had the feeling that she should turn back. She pulled over and adjusted her visor to block the low-hanging sun, but then she got back on the road. The second time she pulled over, she almost turned around. The sun burned her eyes, but it also led her in the right direction.

She realized that she couldn't go back. Virgil would wonder why she was back so soon. She kept driving until she reached Bozeman Blends. When she saw Doug sitting in the coffee shop, she thought she would be nervous, but she was actually alert and aware. Details seemed to take on more weight—the sharp hiss of the coffee boilers, the pulse on Doug's neck, the veins in his hand when he waved to her. Except for the blonde lady making the coffee, Kelly and Doug were alone.

"What will you have?" asked the barista.

"Caramel cappuccino, please."

"I was going to have the same thing," he said.

"Really?" The barista laughed with them as Doug paid for the drinks. The lighthearted friendship made her feel far less nervous. She couldn't remember the last time Virgil had laughed at the same time as her. He found other things to laugh at on TV shows, like bloopers, but he didn't share her sense of humor. It became another wedge that pushed her and Virgil further apart.

She sat down next to him and felt a good kind of chill go through her.

"You've got to see this cabin my family has. You'll enjoy writing up there. I want you to come take a look at it."

Kelly picked up on the subtext right away but tried to keep the conversation casual. "It sounds beautiful. Where is it?" She took a long sip of the cappuccino now that it was cool enough to drink. When she put the cup down, Doug leaned over with his napkin.

"You've got some foam," he said, wiping her upper lip. She knew she was blushing because her cheeks were burning. "It's up in the woods not far from here. My parents own it, but they only use it in the fall when Dad goes hunting. We could stay there and no one would ever know. You'd be free to write all you want. The lake will inspire you; it goes on for miles, and the mountains look blue as the sky up there."

The chance to write without being interrupted sounded wonderful to Kelly. It wasn't what she was planning to do at the cabin, but it made so much sense when he said it. Surrounded by trees in a romantic cabin, she could get so much work done. She took the last drink of the cappuccino. "Let's go then," she said. "We should be finishing our drinks so we can get to work on some writing."

As she walked out of the coffee shop, she realized that Doug had listened to everything she said while she was there, and that the only time he had taken his eyes off her was when he was paying for the coffee. She tried to contrast this with Virgil's habit of staring at the TV and not really listening to her.

She talked to herself when she was following Doug in the Blazer. "Once I cross that bridge, I'm never coming back. I've never done this before." Turning on the radio to occupy her mind, she heard, "My Heart Will Go On" from the movie *Titanic*.

"I don't care," she answered. "I've deprived myself of happiness for too long."

The wedge between Kelly and Virgil went deeper when she looked at the lunchbox resting on the passenger seat, holding the remains of her contract.

When Doug switched on the turn signal on his truck, Kelly followed right along behind him.

When they arrived at Mystic Lake, it was obvious how it earned its name. Through the trees, she glimpsed blue water shining, and where Doug was pulling up ahead of her, there was a simple cabin.

"Let's go down to the lake," said Doug. "It's not dark yet. Would you like to go for a swim?"

"Why not?" she answered.

The world was quiet, except for singing birds in the trees. They were completely alone as they walked.

Doug ran down to the lakeside, quickly pulling his pants off. The air in the mountains was still chilly. What was he doing? As he took off his shirt with equal abandon and raced into the water, skinny-dipping, Kelly stared in surprise. She was completely out her comfort zone.

"Come on, we're just going to have some fun."

Kelly waited, not convinced.

"It'll cool you off, come on."

"I don't have a bathing suit," she answered.

Doug chuckled. "No one's watching."

Kelly slowly took her shirt off, but left her bra on. She took off her jeans. As she was becoming unclothed, he said, "Hurry up!"

She laughed and kept undressing, but she left her underwear on too.

"Come on, what are you waiting for? The water's the perfect temperature."

A nearly full moon was beginning to shine over the lake as she entered the water. The magnificent sunset blazed overhead, turning the water red and blue in varying shades. She had expected purple, but the red and blue stayed two separate colors as she waded in.

Kelly still felt insecure about the whole thing, even though they were alone. But when she walked into the cool water, surrounded by flaming colors and majestic mountains, away from all the dangers of the city far below, she felt free.

For the first time since being trapped with Virgil, she was free. She basked in the blazing colors deepening all around her. She was so enraptured by the moment that she didn't notice Doug until he touched her back.

Kelly didn't realize how much tension she was holding until Doug touched her and she flinched. She focused on breathing away the tension, but Doug kissed her neck, and the surprise of the feeling was too much for her, eliminating her last wisp of hesitation in a rush of desire. She leaned forward, surprised with her own reaction as she craved the known direction his hands were leading, down toward her hips.

Kelly turned around to kiss him and she felt shivers all the way down her legs.

His fingertips gracefully traced her ribs and then teased her nipples, which made her even more sensitive. She couldn't remember Virgil touching her like that, even when they were young and he still looked at her with fondness. She looked at Doug's eyes and saw something more than affection, more than fondness. Doug looked at her with love.

Surrounded by the lake and the sunset, Kelly found herself swept up in the kiss that just kept going and going, like a deep pool of water with no bottom. She felt like she was melting into Doug as all the apprehension left her body.

Wrapped in Doug's arms, she began to notice him shivering against her, and she was starting to get cold too. She searched the heavens, surprised to see how quickly night had fallen. The last vestiges of twilight were disappearing, murky purple auroras dwindling away into the black. She was so far away from the city lights that she could see almost all the stars in the sky.

"I want to stay out here all night," Kelly said.

"So do I," answered Doug.

"You're freezing," Kelly said.

"So are you," Doug said. "We should finish this inside."

They left the water to go back to the cabin and the warmth of the bed awaiting them.

When they arrived, he opened the door for her and let her in, pulling a plastic cover off the couch in front of the fireplace and looking around before saying, "You need to get warm. I need to make a fire."

Kelly watched, enraptured, as Doug carefully loaded kindling and paper into a small pyramid, sparking a flame, and building log after log above the fire.

Once the flames started to heat up, it cleared the cold from her body and sent her into desire again. "Doug?" she asked. He didn't need to answer as he picked her up and carried her into the bedroom.

His warm lips sent chills down her spine. She felt the bed beneath her back, and Doug kissing her on the lips. She started to feel all her walls come down. He took off her bra and panties and he held her hand with gentleness the whole time.

When they were both naked, he slowly rose above her, but the anticipation and suspense increased her need. He brought out feelings she never knew she had. As she felt him get above her and kiss her breasts one at a time, paying extra attention to her nipples, she felt intense heat. He moved down to her belly, and her thighs, and she quietly moaned in ecstasy. Her whole body started to shake. He was even delicate when he entered her. She hadn't expected so much

grace from a strong man like Doug, but his touches continued until she couldn't stop from crying out.

Afterwards, they were lying next to each other, naked,
looking at one another. "You're beautiful. You have nothing
to be ashamed of. You should feel wonderful."

"I've never felt that way, Doug. I didn't feel wonderful
until a few minutes ago."

"What about your stories?"

"A lot of them are old folktales. Even the ones I write
myself are still basically folktales. It's hard to create original
ideas for children's stories."

"Your stories keep children captivated," argued Doug.
"These stories are going to be your future. Especially the story about the dog without a tail. You can't tell me that was
from a folktale."

"You mentioned those agents your father knows. How are
they ever going to notice me? I make short stories, not those
long books."

Doug traced the path of her arm with one finger. "Hey,
they look at children's books too. Do you think those children's books just write themselves? There's always an agent
behind these books, big or small. Everyone needs someone
in their corner. I promise, someday, you'll be standing on a
red carpet, accepting awards for your stories. I knew from
the moment I saw you at the library. It's your destiny."

Kelly leaned in for a kiss, and it wasn't refused. The kiss
stirred up her feelings once more, and it wasn't long before
she was tangled in his embrace.

Chapter Twenty-Six

When she got home, Virgil still didn't pay any attention to her. This still made her happy, but a deep uneasiness suggested to her that his attitude might change.

Back at her writing, Kelly was working on a new story, and she found herself writing much more than usual. She found a text on her phone, alerted by the tiny ding.

You should check out an agent named Homer Zimmerman. We should get together again.

She texted back, **When would be a good time?**

She wanted to get back to her writing, but was too distracted with thoughts of warm embraces in the cool lake. A few minutes later, he texted back. **In a couple days, my wife is going out of town for a few days to see her family in Billings. I could pick you up after story time at the library.**

She was texting back a yes when Virgil walked by. "Texting with Tammy again?" he asked.

"Who else would I be texting?" she asked, and that seemed to make him leave her alone again.

Later that night, when Virgil tried to have sex with her, she found the strength to say no. It was the first time she had been strong enough to say it in twenty years.

Virgil groaned loudly. The smell of beer on his breath was worse than usual, so she observed that he was drinking even more.

"Oh, come on. Why?" he asked.

"You remember that virus I got," she answered.

Virgil looked at her for a second, and said, "Okay. Fine. Sorry I didn't send the mouse outside right away." Then he rolled over on his side and didn't say anything else.

She lay there awake for a long time, thinking about

Doug, the way he touched her, the way he was so sensitive and caring, so different than the way Virgil groped her, treating her like some animal. Doug was actually concerned about her pleasure. As she thought, she felt herself getting aroused all over again. It was difficult for her to fall asleep. She kept thinking about his strong arms embracing her. She managed to fall asleep, but she had no idea what time that was.

When Kelly woke up, she used her cell phone to take a look at Zimmerman's page. He did admit in the bio that not many agents took in children's books anymore, but he also mentioned that children's books were his favorite. This made her really happy, and she decided to send him one of the stories. Along with the contract that she'd hidden in Doug's cabin, this would also give her an agent that could represent her other work so that her stories would continue being published. The contract was only for one of her stories. She had many more that she could turn into children's books.

She quickly printed out *The Dog with No Tail*, and with a sense of urgency, folded up the pages inside an envelope and very carefully addressed it to the agency he worked for. She wrote a cover letter, printed it out as well, and placed it in the envelope before closing it.

Kelly headed down to the post office. The old man who worked there always knew when a story was being sent off.

"Oh, another submission! Excellent! I have a good feeling about this one. Let me kiss it for good luck."

"What would I ever do without you?" she asked. "Your optimism is why I keep sending these stories out there."

He kissed it, and then he held it up for the other workers to see. They came over and kissed it for good luck, too. Kelly smiled and kissed the package one last time as well before handing it over to be mailed, surprised that he'd convinced the other workers to wish her good luck. She'd never entertained the thought that they might genuinely care about her.

Chapter Twenty-Seven

Doug went up to his father Kenneth's house in the rich part of town. The houses were extremely fancy up here. Most of the police and firemen lived up here too. His father acted like he owned the whole town, and Doug could feel his domineering presence the moment he walked out onto the wide front porch. He was tall and skinny, always wearing fancy suits that seemed to make him taller. Today was no exception. He was wearing his Testoni cardigan in style.

"Danielle's been up here talking to me about what you've been doing in your free time. I thought you were hard at work on those condos. I need to talk to you, son!"

Dressed in pink designer shorts and a white button-down shirt, Doug's mother, Francine, stepped out onto the porch sipping a cocktail.

The massive porch gave Doug plenty of room to stay clear of his father. When he was drinking, his father had a tendency to talk with his hands. After too many cocktails, he would even talk with his fists.

"Dad, I just got here and you're shouting already!"

"Listen to your son. Your shouting is giving me a headache, Kenneth." She took a longer sip from the drink.

"I hear you fixed that that Barrett woman's roof for free."

Francine finished her cocktail and was about to head back inside. "You know he's right, Doug. Charity does begin at home. I hope you're still doing right by Danielle."

Doug didn't have a quick answer for his mother, and when she drifted back inside, he was spared from having to think of one.

"You've always been too generous, Doug. You're never going to get anywhere being so nice to people. Why do you care if people have leaks in their roofs? Doesn't it help clean them off?"

His father's entitled attitude bothered him more than usual that day, and he couldn't help but fight back.

"But you should have seen her roof, Dad! It was leaking everywhere. You would have done the same thing!" Doug took a couple of steps toward his father.

Francine stopped in her tracks, and the tone of her voice was so high that Doug knew his mother didn't have a headache, or else she would be making it worse with that screaming. "That's horrible! No one should ever have to live with water dripping on their heads. Have you ever heard of water torture? He's just being a decent human being. I should let you sleep in the rain for a couple days."

"Oh, Francine, you know I'd never let you live in a run-down house. Have you noticed the roofers coming over every year to replace the tar?"

Kenneth took a step forward before putting his drink on one of the railings. He took another step forward, closing the distance between him and the lawn chairs on the porch.

"I built my construction business from the ground up, and now you're just using it to do free work. I didn't get here by working for free, and if I had been willing to do that, I wouldn't have gotten paid. What makes you so special?"

Doug started to lose his temper. To make a point, he took another step forward and sat down in a lawn chair. "Because I'm not like you, Dad. I'm not an asshole!"

"I'm proud of being an asshole," answered Kenneth. "How do you think I've made so much money? By not giving in when people didn't want to pay me. I'd rather be an asshole than live in poverty. You must be in love with that bitch or something."

Francine walked over to Kenneth's drink and threw it over the railing of the porch before aiming a slap at his face. "Kenneth! That's enough! No woman deserves to be called that."

Kenneth caught his wife's hand before she could strike him and pushed her arm away. "I can call that no-good bitch whatever I want."

Doug could feel his temper boiling, but tried to stay out of the fight between his parents.

Kenneth was losing ground against Francine, so he

turned to face Doug.

"Well, son, are you screwing her or not?"

This time, Francine's slap connected. As Kenneth stood still, dumbfounded, Doug realized it was time to make his point before his father's narcissism could return.

"How can you even accuse me of something like that? She's a human being. She deserves compassion. But no, Dad, you always think the worst of me, don't you? You know what? I can't take any more of your insults."

Feeling that he'd made his point, Doug walked back to his truck.

"You're not a Carlton anymore," shouted Kenneth from the porch. "You'd better change your name!"

Chapter Twenty-Eight

Kelly drove over to Tammy's house, which was almost as organized as the library. She had many bookshelves, and many tables for reading, but never once bought a television. She had invested in a coffeemaker. She brought over two cups of coffee. "What did you want to talk to me about?"

Kelly drank the hot coffee, wondering what to say. "I feel like such a horrible person. I did something awful."

"What did you do?" Tammy asked at once.

Kelly had to drink more coffee. "It was so terrible. I had an affair! I cheated on Virgil!"

"With Doug?"

"How did you know?" Kelly almost choked.

"Well, it's not like that makes you a terrible person. I saw all the signs, Kelly. I knew you were in a loveless relationship for a long time. You can't cheat on someone that you don't love anymore."

"I feel awful. Virgil's always been good to me!"

"Good to you? If any other guy loved you, he would have tried to provide for you a little harder, wouldn't he? He makes you live in that run-down house with all the dripping leaks in the ceiling. The Chinese used dripping water for torture for thousands of years. The way he neglects you is tantamount to abuse!"

"The roof doesn't leak anymore, by the way," said Kelly. "Doug fixed it."

"Well, thank God for that. I'm glad you don't have to listen to that dripping anymore."

"Yeah, but what about Doug's wife? What about her? I didn't see her until the dance. They have children! They have kids, Tammy! It just makes me nervous about the whole thing."

"There's nothing to worry about. People cheat all the time. Everyone wants to be happy."

Kelly had a different point of view, but she tried to agree. "I guess you're right, but it's not just his wife that I'm worried about. I know Virgil is going to be angry when he finds out, and he's got a right to be."

Tammy leaned forward, concern on her face. "He doesn't have any right to be angry at you, Kelly. You were in the hospital for five weeks because of that mouse, and we really missed you at the library. Virgil actually talked to me about that situation while you were at the hospital. He told me that he kept taking care of that mouse for weeks, and it never bit him once. But I don't care what Virgil says. If that virus had killed you, I would have made him pay for it."

"He didn't tell you what else he did that day?"

Tammy laughed. "Besides deciding to name the mouse Hector?"

"He actually tore up a contract for 'The Fox and the Crow.' I just managed to get it mailed in the other day. If he hadn't torn it up, then I would have had that advance money months ago."

Tammy's reaction was more shocking than she expected. "I would have slit his throat if he did that to me. Being a librarian might give me a bias, but I'm passionate about books."

Kelly felt some relief, and laughed about her last comment. She tried to relax, but one by one her worries kept popping into her mind.

"I'm trying to be serious, though. I'm worried that he'll try to stop me again. What if he looks at the mail and finds the check before I do?"

"Don't even tell him about the money, Kelly. In fact, you can put it in a different bank account, so he never even sees it. And if he tries to stop you from leaving, just hit him in the balls and make a run for it. You just have to make sure everything is packed first."

Kelly made a mental list of the things she wanted to take with her, but it seemed like a short enough list that she wouldn't even have to write it down.

"I don't have a lot of things to pack anyway, just my typewriter and my stories. Everything else can wait. Oh, by the way, do you know what Danielle did?"

"Wait," said Tammy. "Who is Danielle now?"

Kelly realized she'd never even mentioned Doug's wife, and she realized that Tammy had never even seen Danielle at the barn dance.

"That's Doug's wife. She called me a charity case at the barn dance. I hate it when people call me that. Maybe I don't have a lot of possessions, but it's not like I'm on welfare or something."

"You really have to stop worrying about how other people feel about you, Kelly. It's like you're not even putting yourself as the top priority. You know as well as I do that back in high school women would get pregnant just so they could keep the hot boyfriend. Remember Sally?"

"How could I ever forget Sally?" she asked. She wanted to admit that she hadn't thought about Sally since she'd been in high school, but she felt like that would be rude.

Her boyfriend wanted to break up with her because she was Catholic and he was Protestant, but she got pregnant and he was rich and now they're still married! Men can get just as trapped in relationships as women can. I wonder where they are now."

"That part is true, Tammy." A chill ran down her back. "How did you know that? You're the only one I can talk to about this. Please don't tell anyone."

"You know me. I'm more than capable of keeping secrets. Who would I tell?" She laughed. "So...are you going to see him again?"

"I'm planning on meeting Doug this weekend. I can't seem to tear myself away from him. I feel...drawn to him. Do you know what I mean?"

"Well, Kelly, you know I'm not the one to judge that. I've been divorced twice. You have to follow your heart."

Kelly appreciated the validation. "My heart says this is the way. I told Virgil I was going to be with you this weekend. I hope you don't mind."

"Now you want me to lie for you? Well, it doesn't matter, because Virgil never calls me anyway." Tammy's phone rang. She answered it, and listened carefully. "I'm sorry, Kelly. They need me at the library. I'm supposed to be helping out at the Fall Fundraiser. I've got to get going."

***

When she got home, Virgil was already in a bad mood. "Where were you today? I tried to make dinner for you, just to make you happy, and now you show up late!"

"Sorry, Virgil. What did you cook?" She knew the apology wasn't normal for her, but she hoped that he would miss it.

"Mac and cheese," Virgil said without looking up.

"My favorite!" Kelly answered.

They ate in silence, Virgil still steaming about something. But Kelly knew Virgil couldn't hold his tongue for very long. Soon, he started snapping, and Kelly stopped eating so she could defend herself.

"I found a three-hundred-dollar bill from that knickknack place, *Fingerhut* —three hundred dollars? How am I supposed to pay that kind of money?"

Kelly took a long moment. "Well, I was going to pay them back a little bit at a time."

"You didn't look at the bill. It's behind by three months! Do you know what the interest is on that?"

"What about your job? Isn't that bringing in some money?"

Virgil picked up his coffee cup and hurled it across the table. Kelly ducked, prepared. The coffee missed her, and the cup slammed into the wall. Kelly stared at the wall in shock. The ceramic cup shattered, and black coffee was dripping down the wall.

"Are you insane? You could have killed me!"

Virgil answered, "Since you're still alive, aren't you going to clean that up?"

"If you think I'm cleaning that up, you *are* insane." Kelly carried the typewriter into the bedroom so she could write and calm down. She decided to text Doug as well.

He's yelling because I bought some stuff from a catalogue and now the bills are coming due.

She went back to work on her story until Doug texted her back.

Just tell him it's going to be paid for. He doesn't have to know about your advance. Just mention the hospital in Billings.

Doug's text brought relief to her shoulders. Virgil would calm down as soon as she explained that the debt would be taken care of, and that was enough for her.

Kelly went back to typing, but she couldn't resist the urge to answer him. His answer was so encouraging that she couldn't hold onto the tension anymore.

That's a wonderful idea.

Doug's reassuring answers soothed her, so she went back and forth between the typewriter and the phone. It was easier for her to focus with an understanding person giving her advice.

That night, once Virgil closed his eyes, he started to snore, and Kelly shut off her own light as quietly as possible. She scooted under the covers so she wouldn't wake him up. She stayed awake for several hours, thinking about Doug touching her skin with tender gestures, and how his sensitive fingers brought a thrill running down her arms when he touched her shoulders.

Chapter Twenty-Nine

Kelly was working on a story when she got a phone call. "This is Denise from the Children's Hospital in Billings. My friend Becky brought her daughter to story time last Wednesday. She said your stories were just fantastic, and I thought the children here would love it if you could come and read for them. Do you think you can be here in an hour?"

"Sure," she said. "I could make it in about an hour."

Kelly headed to Billings right away. When she arrived, Denise noticed her. "If you can do this on a regular basis, I can give you fifty dollars each time."

"That would help so much," she said. "I work at the library on a regular basis. That would be very fun." She noticed Doug sitting in the lobby. He was all by himself, looking back and forth. She turned to Denise. "Could you excuse me for a few minutes?"

Denise nodded, and Kelly went over to Doug. Just seeing him agitated made her want to go over and comfort him. She began to realize that she was falling in love with him. She had felt the need to comfort Virgil from time to time, but that had passed years ago.

"Doug, what are you doing here? Are your children okay?"

"They're fine."

Kelly sighed in relief.

"It's actually my friend Betty's kid, Sally. What are you doing here?"

"I got invited to read my stories to the children. They're even paying me. So it's your friend Betty's kid?"

"She's here because she was camping with her family down at Yellowstone. She was going too fast on her bicycle and ended up crashing in the woods. She was closer to

Billings, so they brought her here for observation. And when they X-rayed her, they found out she broke her arm and her leg too. She's never had to have a cast before."

"That's horrible. I hope she gets better. What room is she in? I don't mind reading the story twice. It would cheer her up."

"Kelly?" said Denise behind her. "The children are waiting for you."

Kelly turned to Denise. "After you," she said. "I've never been here before."

Denise went off down one of the green hallways and Kelly followed her. Inside, she could hear the kids clapping already, and when she entered, she noticed all the children instantly turn their heads to look at her, even the ones in wheelchairs. "Story time!" they said.

"Children, say hello to Kelly."

"Hi, Kelly," came the chorus of high-pitched voices.

"Kelly is going to read you some stories. She will be reading here again, if you're nice to her."

"We promise!" cheered the kids.

Kelly said, "This is an old Italian story. Once upon a time, there were three sisters living in Italy. The youngest and most beautiful daughter was called Ella, but her two older sisters were not as pretty, and they were constantly disdainful of her and making fun of her. They made her work the hardest around the house and called her Cinderella."

As the children listened to her story, giggling as she moved the invisible sponge around in the air, and laughing out loud when she pouted and snorted like the jealous sisters, she noticed Doug come in.

Doug stayed by the door and watched.

As he watched her move like the mice, and then like the horses they turned into, he noticed that her body was coming alive every time she acted out the story. He found himself falling even more in love with her, lost in the story until the children all clapped. Then he caught hold of himself and started clapping too.

After she was done reading, she walked over to Doug. "I'd like to read to Sally now," she said.

Doug led her to the girl's room. Sally's leg was in a full cast, hanging in the air and leaving her bedridden. Her arm was in a big cast too, so she couldn't really move at all.

"Sally," said Doug, "Kelly's going to read you a story."

Kelly wanted to tell the Cinderella story again, but when she saw Sally, she knew she had to read *The Dog with No Tail*. When she got done reciting her story, Sally had a genuine smile on her face.

Chapter Thirty

Three days later, Doug invited her back to the cabin at Mystic Lake. Doug was waiting for her there with a bottle of wine.

As she was going through the cabin, she noticed that books of poetry from the likes of Sylvia Plath and Walt Whitman. She never would have expected him to read poetry.

Kelly and Doug sat on the porch, sipping wine while birds sang all around. The peaceful scenery set her mind at ease.

Doug finished his wine and poured another glass while asking, "Why did you get into writing?"

"When I was very young, my parents would take me over to my grandmother's house up in Great Falls. She used to read all kinds of stories to me."

"My father was in construction, working on the biggest projects, but before he did all that, he was a writer himself. I never wanted for anything, so I had time to dive into Shakespeare, Keats, Milton, and all the other great poets. I loved reading my entire life. When I'm not working on a house, I'm usually here reading poetry. You are a wonderful storyteller."

They drank iced tea once the wine was all gone.

"You love children so much. How come you don't have any kids of your own?"

"After I married Virgil, I got pregnant, but I had a miscarriage because I fell off a stepladder."

"Why were you on a stepladder when you were pregnant? Virgil should have been doing all the work."

"I was hanging pictures on the wall. It just seemed like an accident, but the doctor said I also had an infection in my ovaries. I might not ever be able to have kids."

"There are more important things in the world than having kids. It's far more important that you're being positive instead of dwelling on the past. I've fallen in love with you, Kelly."

"I wish this day could go on forever. You're so much nicer than Virgil. I don't ever want to go home." She kissed him passionately, and he brought her inside. She jumped in his arms and started kissing him again. He carried her into the bedroom, still wrapped around him, and she started getting her shirt off as she got on the bed. Then she went back to kissing him. She got in front of him and gently rocked up and down. They both reached their peak at the same time.

Days ago, Kelly had dug up the box with the ruined contract and brought it up to Mystic Lake. She had wanted to make sure she could trust Doug first, but now that she knew he was looking out for her, she knew she was able to.

She brought it out from under the bed where she'd kept it hidden and brought it into the living room. The small box sat in her lap with very little weight, and she opened it just to make sure that the pieces were still there. In spite of the lightness of the box, hundreds of scraps of paper stared back at her. It was a monumental task.

Doug was already looking at the box and, when she closed it again, he said, "What's in there?"

Instantly, she opened it again and removed the pieces of the contract. "This is a contract for my children's book. Virgil tore it up, but if I can get it put back together, they might let me still publish my book there."

"He tore it apart? When was this?"

"Right after Virgil started working for you. He just tore the entire thing to shreds and said it was a scam."

"It's a lot more money than he's making doing construction work for my company. Why would he deprive you of a good future?"

Kelly didn't want to spell it out, but Doug had proved that he was willing to listen to her.

"Because if I don't make any money off my books, it's kind of hard to get away, you know, with down payments and everything."

"Ridgewood and Sons is not a phony company. They're one of the oldest houses in New York. They even print the *New Yorker*. Even my father, the great writer, has submitted his book there. You scored really big with this one."

"But it's all torn up. What if they don't accept it like that? Virgil always does this to me. He takes away everything I ever loved. He took away my dog. I had a dog named Houdini for a long time, but Virgil left the front door open and he got hit by a car. That dog even saved me from a rattlesnake. He took away my roses. We had rosebushes, but he watered them too much. He even took away my contract. Virgil destroys everything!" Kelly broke down in tears, and even though anger flooded her, it was regret that brought the tears. Months of waiting and looking for some type of vengeance was something that left her with regret. If she had been living alone, she would have signed the contract.

"Don't cry, don't worry. I know we have some transparent tape lying around here somewhere. We'll get this contract put back together. Don't let that awful excuse for a man get the last laugh. You deserve this."

Slowly but surely, Doug and Kelly taped the shreds of paper, page by page, until the entire contract was assembled. They connected the words together, back and forth, putting the margins together first.

Kelly tried to stay calm, but she had a lot of anger built up, which was now turning into excitement because everything was finally going to change for her.

"This is definitely the first page. This is the part with the number," said Doug.

"Here's a three, and a four, and a seven," said Kelly. She started to organize the numbers on the table, and assembled the pages from the top down while Doug worked on the other side

They had gotten seven sheets of the contract completed.

"This advance is fifteen thousand dollars, Kelly."

"Are you sure? Virgil said that the advance comes out of my money from the book sales. It's basically a rip-off."

"He probably never told you that you're earning sixty percent off each book sold."

"I did notice that part," she answered. "But if that advance takes the money before I sell the books, how do I know that it's all going to work out?"

"Don't you know how many people buy children's books? Everyone with kids."

With only a few pieces left on the other sheets, Kelly

looked up at Doug. "What if they don't like the fact that it's been ripped up?" Fear began to grip her again.

"Don't worry," Doug said. "I've seen worse things happen to contracts. They're still going to accept it."

Kelly breathed deeply and tried to relax. It was difficult putting the pieces together when she was stressed out. When she calmed down, it was easier to connect the broken words, and the numbered sections of the contract made it easier to figure out. With the entire contract spread out in front of her, Kelly could read about the team of lawyers that would protect her rights and understood that the contract really was a good deal.

"I'm so happy. Virgil didn't give me time to finish reading the contract, much less sign it."

"They're definitely not con artists. I know some of them personally. They'd never rip you off."

Soon, all 14 pages of the contract were back together again.

"This contract doesn't have an expiration date. Sometimes, they're only valid for a couple months, then you miss out."

Taping everything together one piece at a time had taken all day, and the sun was setting through the trees over Mystic Lake. The sunset was a brilliant red and flashed in the lake like fire.

"Just sign here and *The Fox and the Crow* will be in print in a few months, once they iron out all the details. In the meantime, you can live off that advance."

Kelly paused with the pen over the contract. Then she signed her name on the line and dated it. Doug got an envelope and they prepared the package. She dropped the envelope in her purse.

"I want to mail this off as soon as I can," she said. "It's getting dark already. Crap, the post office is closed. Virgil is going to see the contract before I can get it mailed off."

Doug chuckled. "Don't go home then. Just spend the night here, Kelly."

"Yes, that does seem like a better idea," she answered.

Chapter Thirty-One

Returning home the next morning, Kelly found Virgil in the kitchen instead of the living room. "Where have you been? You were gone all night!"

"I had a girl's night out with Tammy. You don't mind, do you?"

Virgil was looking directly at her this time. Instead of ignoring her, he was paying attention. This told her right away that something had changed.

"I think you've been spending way too much time with that librarian. Are you sure you haven't been cheating on me? Did you find an attractive doctor over there in Billings?"

This had been one of Kelly's worst-case scenarios when thinking about spending time with Doug. The fear that had been troubling her since she started getting attracted to Doug came to life before her, and she had to blink to stay focused. The easiest way she had figured out was to completely deny it, and this was the first thing she went for.

"With who?" she asked. She had thought up several excuses as she was going through with everything.

"You turned me down for sex the other night. What was that all about?"

"Really? Ever since that Hantavirus incident, I haven't been in the mood. And why are you so sensitive all of a sudden?"

After weeks in the hospital, this seemed like the perfect point to make.

"We've been fighting! We barely even talk! What's going on?"

Kelly started to lose her temper, and more anger started to pour out.

"Virgil, it's not the 1970s anymore! Women have rights these days. Oh, that's right, you're not able to think at that level. You can't just have sex with me whenever you want. I've had a long day and I need some sleep! I'm going to bed. By myself." Kelly shut the bedroom door and locked it tight.

Virgil rattled the doorknob. "Did you just lock the door on me?"

"Hey, you're not the only one who lives here. If you recall, you made me sleep on the couch. That's how I got the mouse bite, remember? The Hantavirus? Remember? You'd better get comfortable out there, because I'm going to sleep!"

Kelly hoped the tirade would force Virgil to leave her alone. After all, she did want to get some sleep, but more importantly, she wanted to keep Virgil from seeing her face. The strain of trying to hide her feelings about Doug was starting to weigh on her, especially now that the argument had become a question of her faithfulness.

She knew that her expression was radiating fear, and she didn't want Virgil to see that. She used her anger as a false front, yelling and carrying on and hoping that Virgil would actually leave her alone. Inside, she was worried that Virgil would see her tension, or that he might pick up on the difference between the two expressions. As she hid in the bedroom, she kept building up her anger, her frustration at having to hide in her own bedroom, and her anger at Virgil for not backing down.

"You just locked the door on me. All right, you asked for it."

Kelly started to breathe faster, because she knew exactly what Virgil was talking about. When Virgil started to talk like that, he was about to get physical. She immediately stood up and backed away from the inward-swinging door so she wouldn't be in the way. She backed up against the far wall, bracing her back and squaring her shoulders.

She knew it wouldn't happen instantly, because Virgil was still gathering air for the kick. It was a throwback from his football days where he had to gather oxygen to maintain the block or run down the field when he was a wide receiver. She'd had to learn a few things about football after listening to his rants about quarterback salaries and everything. She didn't care for the sport, but her knowledge gave her a good idea of how to defend herself. She was already remembering different tackle positions where it was easier to push an opponent to the side instead of head-on, since it would push him into the wall instead of her.

As she prepared for the fight, she realized why he was building up so much air. He wasn't about to dry-punch the door; he was going to bring the whole thing down. Her heart pounded as the seconds crawled past.

Kelly waited in suspense for a few seconds before Virgil slammed the door right off the hinges with a full charge, tearing the door free. It flew across the room and the hinges held it back for half a second, making it crash into the closet instead of into Kelly, where she stood behind the bed with her back to the wall.

"Virgil! What's wrong with you?"

"This is my house. You don't lock me out of my own bedroom!"

"You don't get to throw cups of coffee at me! You don't get to ruin our house. Who cares if we own it? You still can't break the door down like that."

The anger had moved into full steam. All her confidence was built up for the moment. She knew that he was crossing the line, and she knew that she had a right to put him in his place. She knew that her display was starting to convince Virgil that she was being honest, because his hands were starting to shake a lot. Every time he got scared, his hands would start to shake, and every time he got angry, he'd be all calm and collected, something Kelly thought of as being cool as a cucumber.

"Oh, come on," he said. "I'm sorry I ruined your door. Can't I sleep in here with you tonight?"

"The way you're acting, I've seen bulls that have more feelings than you!"

Kelly's rage was soaring. She pointed her finger out the now-empty doorway and Virgil was starting to look genuinely scared. She didn't want to push him too far, but he had made some serious attempts to terrify her and she wasn't about to put up with any more of it. If she did tolerate it, she knew that it was only a matter of time before Virgil would start hitting her. The rage that had burned through him as he destroyed the door assured her of his sadistic intentions.

"I'm not sleeping in the same room as you tonight! But I'm not sleeping on the couch, oh no, Virgil, that's definitely not happening. Not ever again. You get out of this bedroom right now! And I don't want to hear one more word out of you tonight. For crying out loud, if you were a child, you'd be in time-out for weeks, that stunt you pulled. And get that door out of the closet on your way out! I don't want that reminder sitting in our closet all night."

Virgil took the door out of the closet without a word. The bulky piece of wood was not easy for him to maneuver out the doorway, but he only grunted in effort a few times and did not say a word to her, just like she'd asked.

Kelly tried to get some sleep, but the morning sun woke her bright and early. She was awake by the time Virgil left for work, leaving the couch without a word.

She texted Doug. **Virgil and I had a big fight last night. He accused me of cheating, but I made him regret it. He slept on the couch last night. He broke the bedroom door right off the hinges. He was ready to start a fistfight, but I chased him off.**

Doug texted back. **I'll make sure he pays for that. I'm his boss. Thanks for warning me.**

Chapter Thirty-Two

Doug didn't want to admit to himself that the text from Kelly shook him.

Doug watched Virgil pull up to the job site several minutes later. He was driving too fast and he slammed the door of his Blazer. Doug crossed his arms defensively.

Virgil went over to Doug at once. "I've got bills to pay," he said. "I want to do something else besides painting."

"Sure, I can put you to work. All these windows need framing."

Virgil nodded. "Yeah, that doesn't look too hard."

Doug slapped Virgil on the shoulder in a friendly way, but he wanted to drop a hard punch and leave a bruise. "You can do it, buddy! Just make sure all the corner cuts are clean before you lay down the trim. And use those half-inch screws. Nothing to it, Virgil."

Doug laid on the charm as he talked, but inside, he was boiling just as much as Kelly.

Virgil nodded and headed into the first condo while Doug stayed by his truck and sent other workers to their tasks. He made frequent trips to his truck to check the text messages.

Doug went into the condo to see how Virgil was doing. Inside, he noticed that only three windows were done and, even then, the screws were sticking out of the trim.

"Virgil, Virgil, what are you doing?"

"What? These are half-inch screws."

The other workers were paying attention to Doug, turning off their power tools so they could hear the conversation.

"You have to get the trim flush against the wall. Every time you don't screw it in all the way, it makes it harder to install the inner pane. Look what happens when I try to slide it in place."

Doug lifted one of the square glass panes, and when he slid it along the trim pieces, the screw heads prevented the pane from going into place.

"You're going to have to start over, but these rectangle windows are going to be a start-from-scratch. All of these side pieces are too short. That's for the top of the windows, not the side."

"I noticed they were pretty short," said Virgil. The chuckling from the other workers became louder.

"Then why did you even put them up?"

Virgil started to stutter, and the other workers cracked up.

"Get back to work!" said Doug. The workers resumed their duties without a response.

When Doug bought his lunch pail out, the workers filed out of the house and took a lunch break too. Doug's lunch pail was their cue that it was time for their lunch breaks. Virgil sat close to Doug.

"I think my wife is having an affair. She's turning me down for sex. Do you know who she might be sleeping with?" Each one of their comments was punctuated by large bites from their sandwiches. Virgil had a bologna sandwich, but Doug was able to afford pastrami for his lunchmeat.

Doug was surprised that Virgil would be so upfront about it, but he'd had all morning to prepare. He laughed, waving his arm to dismiss the question. "Me? Why would I know? I've got no idea if she's sleeping around."

"Well, you're a big-time contractor and all, so you know a lot of people, right? You must have heard something."

"Not those kind of people. I don't hang around with low-lifes."

"Are you saying my friends are lowlifes?"

"I'm trying to tell you that I'm not the kind of guy that sleeps around. I've already got two kids to worry about."

Doug thought back to the texts he'd been getting from Kelly. *Virgil almost hit Kelly last night and he's trying to act like the wounded party here.*

"I know she's sleeping with somebody else, but I just don't know who it is. Not yet, anyway. But the little bastard is going to be sorry."

"Has Kelly ever made you so mad that you hit her?" he

asked.

Virgil shook his head, but after a deep breath, he admitted, "I did throw a can of chili at her one time. But I am an adult, you know. I realize that it was wrong to hurt her."

"Well, you did admit that you did something wrong. Maybe she hasn't forgiven you for that yet."

"She is angry, I'll give you that. But wouldn't that make her more likely to cheat on me?"

You actually hit a woman, Virgil. How can you call yourself an adult? It's just childish.

Doug tried to think things out before his next comment.

He looked at Virgil eye to eye. "Look, Virgil, here's the thing. Your wife reads stories to children all the time. It's the joy of her life. I can't imagine her doing something like cheat on you."

Virgil had a defiant look in his eyes, but he backed down. "We'll see," he said.

Virgil only had a couple bites left by the time Doug was done with his sandwich. He started putting things back in his lunch pail.

"Why don't you try plumbing? It's just big pipes and glue. That shouldn't be too challenging."

Doug led Virgil back inside, pointing at the larger pipe under the floor beams. Since the plumbing was unfinished, the floor was still an array of beams crisscrossing like a series of stepping stones. "I need you to get all the copper tubes in place. Just don't use this line for the water. The big line is the city sewer line." He pointed at the smaller pipe. "This is the water inlet line. Make sure you only use this one when you're hooking up the copper."

"Got it," said Virgil. "I'm using the smaller pipe."

Doug climbed the stairs, monitoring work on the second floor. Ten minutes later, he heard a bloodcurdling scream and ran downstairs.

Virgil was sitting on the floor. He'd attached the pipe to the sewer line, but the other end was attached to the bottom of the sink. Water continued to spray out of the sink, drenching the cupboards, the stove, and Virgil himself.

"What were you thinking? I have to replace all these kitchen fixtures!"

Virgil looked defeated, but he still had a quick answer for

Doug. "Why can't I just scrub the counters down?" he asked.

"Because they're contaminated. That's sewer water dripping off of you. That's thousands of dollars you just cost me! I thought you said you had some experience in plumbing!"

"I do have experience in plumbing. You told me to do the wrong thing on purpose, didn't you?"

This was the last straw for Doug. "I told you not to make any attachments to the big pipe. We already have outlet valves on the copper pipe. You just cost me thousands of dollars, and you can't even take responsibility. Just get out of here. Don't even think about coming back, because you're fired." He stood his ground as Virgil got off the beams and walked out the door without a word. He stood at the front door and made sure Virgil drove away before heading back into the condo.

Chapter Thirty-Three

Six long weeks brought a new season to Bozeman, and snow drifted out of the sky, pulled from the air by the tall Rocky Mountains. Along with the snow, a change in the old mailman's habits emerged again. Instead of walking, he drove a small car from mailbox to mailbox. He moved much quicker in his car than he did on foot, so Kelly was happy to see him drive by.

She pulled her snow boots on before she walked outside. They didn't fit too well, but they got her to the mailbox.

The first letter was from Ridgewood and Sons, and it was written by the illustrator for her new book. The woman doing Kelly's pictures had been nice enough to include some examples of her artwork, and the laughing crow looked almost lifelike to her.

Underneath the letter from the illustrator, she also found the advance check inside the envelope. She got even happier when she saw that, but she had a hard time tearing her eyes away from the beautiful illustrations. Neil wasn't paying her a lot of attention, but Virgil could still see the check, and she wasn't going to take any chances.

Inside was a letter from the Dove Literary Agency. The agent had scribbled an XOX on the envelope. Instead of going back through the snow and opening the letter inside, Kelly opened it immediately.

Dear Kelly Barrett,

This is Homer Zimmerman, from the Dove Literary Agency. I have read your submission very carefully several times. The other agents here have read it, too. It is with great pleasure that I would like to announce that we all think

you're an incredible writer. I'd like to take you on immediate-
ly. Please sign the enclosed contract at your soonest conven-
ience if you're all right with the terms.

Regards and congratulations,

Homer Zimmerman

Kelly had been waiting her entire life for this. Ever since she had started writing stories and telling them to children, she had always dreamed of the day when parents all over could be reading her stories—not Dr. Seuss or R.L. Stine, but her own stories—to their young children at night. She felt happier than she ever had in her life. She started dancing around in the snow, kicking up flurries of snowflakes with her boots, covering her coat in snow. She didn't care. She just kept on dancing and laughing regardless.

Next door, Neil stared at her, perplexed. He stuck his head out the window. "What in the world has gotten into your silly little head now?"

"I got published, I got published," sang Kelly.

"They finally didn't send you a rejection letter?" said Neil, lifting his head in surprise. He banged into the window. "Ouch!" he cried. "Look what you made me do!" The bump from his head dislodged snow from his roof, and it plummet-ed down and smacked him on the head. He pulled his head back inside and muttered a long string of words she couldn't quite hear, but Kelly was still dancing and laughing.

Chapter Thirty-Four

Virgil was driving Kelly home from the library the next day because he could handle the ice on the road a lot better than she could. Kelly was smiling because some people had wanted her to read a special story to their children, one of her own favorites called *Goodnight Moon*. Virgil, however, was not smiling.

"What's wrong with you these days, Kelly?" Virgil was spitting the words out between gritted teeth. "It's like you've been avoiding me lately."

"No, Virgil, that's not true! I've just been so busy at the library! There are so many children that want to hear my stories now."

"And I guess you've been getting too friendly with the parents, haven't you? That's why you get back here all flustered and breathless, isn't it? Who is it this time?"

"Virgil! What are you talking about?"

Virgil started driving faster. "You've been cheating, haven't you?"

Even though it was true, Kelly still felt every ounce of rage at being accused of it. "Never, Virgil! I would never do that to you! Especially not when I'm reading stories to the kids."

"Oh, really? You get all hot and flustered, sweaty and blushing, and you're telling me it's just the weather?"

Kelly hadn't noticed that she'd been blushing that much. She touched her cheeks and they were burning hot.

"You've been gone way more than usual. Sometimes, I even get home before you! I've been working long days on these condos and you're still getting home after me? The library doesn't stay open that late, Kelly. Think about it! I checked it out myself. They close at four, okay? You're getting home at nine some nights! Gone all night that one time! This isn't right and you know it! You've been seeing someone, I swear!"

"No, Virgil, I haven't!"

Virgil raced down the avenue, where the people's houses hung back from the street, guarded by picket fences. Children were building snowmen in the front yards, and she thought she was safe.

"Get out of the car!" he yelled.

"But we're still moving!" Kelly yelled back at him.

"I don't care, you slut! Get out of my car right now!"

Kelly froze. No one had ever forced her out of a car before and she had no idea how to deal with the new situation.

Virgil turned to scowl at her. He slowed down and got to the side of the road. First, he popped her seatbelt and it came loose at once. Then he reached out one arm to open her side door. Kelly had enough time to look at Virgil in shock as she felt herself being thrown. She didn't realize that he was capable of this. A can of chili was one thing, but now she experienced true violence.

During the jolt, Kelly felt like her insides were being shoved around. As she lost her balance and tumbled out of the moving Blazer, she tried to brace for the impact with the road, but she only had a moment. Her body landed against the pavement. The pain was intense for a moment, and the landing knocked the wind out of her.

She grunted and tried to sit up, noticing pain lingering her elbow.

The kids that had been making snowmen had vanished, but their parents had come outside, standing in the snow and talking on their cell phones. Kelly wondered who they were talking to.

One of the parents got close enough for Kelly to hear her. The mother was talking on the phone still, and she was saying "I just saw this woman get thrown out of a moving car, Operator."

Kelly realized that the mother was talking to the police. Virgil had finally gone too far, but it wasn't until then that she realized something was going to be done about it. Kelly continued to try and catch her breath. The ice on the roadway seemed to make the impact even harder on her body.

She started to get up, but the slick ice made the process much more strenuous. By this time, Virgil had stopped the car long enough to lean over so he could grab the open passenger door and swing it shut from the inside.

As Virgil stopped the car, Kelly saw Doug walking past her, heading toward them. She hadn't even seen his truck earlier, but she had been too fixed on arguing with Virgil and too distracted by being shoved out of the car. As Virgil reached out to grab the door handle, Doug caught up to him and grabbed his wrist.

Doug pulled Virgil out of the car and threw him to the ground.

"Don't even think about getting up," said Doug as Virgil tried to get to his feet.

"She's my woman," said Virgil. "I can do whatever I want to her."

"No, you can't," answered Doug. He stood over Virgil, and whenever Virgil tried to move toward the car, he would stand in his way again.

"That really hurt," complained Virgil.

"What demon possessed you to throw Kelly out of a car?" asked Doug. "She's hurting a lot worse than you."

"She's been cheating on me," he answered.

"Can you blame her? You don't even deserve her if you're going to treat her like that. I'm going to take her somewhere else where you can never hurt her again."

"You can't do this," complained Virgil. "I'll stop you!"

Doug went over to his truck at once, returning with some rope. Before Virgil could even get to his feet, Doug had his hands bound up.

"Get your things and hop in the truck," said Doug.

Kelly went to the backseat of the car and retrieved her contracts and her stories. Her advance check was already in her purse, so all she had to do was grab the stories and her purse before she was ready to leave.

"You can't get away with this," said Virgil.

"You can't get away with throwing a woman out of a moving car," he answered.

Kelly got into Doug's truck, and they sped off down the road while police cars approached from behind them to apprehend Virgil. Despite the cold weather, Kelly felt the need to roll the window down. The wind blew her long hair around, and she felt like she was finally free.

Chapter Thirty-Five

Doug headed down the freeway while Kelly rolled up the window. The wind was starting to make her feel colder.

She rubbed her elbow as the truck sped into the Rocky Mountains. The experience of driving over the snow-covered mountains was much less treacherous than the journey made by Lewis and Clark and their band of explorers, but she felt no less amazed by the passing ridges and glaciers as they headed toward Idaho.

"Where should we go?" asked Doug.

"I think Seattle is far enough away. Besides, my sister lives there."

"I'm fine with that," said Doug.

"What about your parents?"

"They didn't see Virgil throw you out of the car, so they wouldn't understand me anyway."

Kelly tried to rephrase it. She knew that the fighting in his family ran much deeper than that. "How will your parents handle your leaving everything behind, your job, your family?"

Doug brushed the bristles on his chin, pondering, but kept his eyes on the road, scanning for black ice and down-shifting for passing vehicles.

"They'll just get someone else to finish building those condos. Besides, I can get much better work out there in Seattle. They never stop building over there."

Kelly wanted to express how much it meant to her, but when she opened her mouth, she said, "I want an apartment where I can see the water."

Doug laughed. "All the apartments have a view of the water in Seattle. That won't be hard to find at all."

Seattle welcomed her like a new chance at life. She

knew that not everyone got these second chances, and she was determined to make the most of it.

The sound that went on for miles and miles kept a calm atmosphere over the town that nestled on the hills rising out of the peaceful harbor. Despite the cranes hanging from sky-scrapers and bulldozers clearing new land for fresh houses, the Seattle before her seemed to be at ease.

Even when she found the building with an apartment above a place that she would use as a bookstore, she felt the same peaceful energy, but she also picked up a wave of ex-citement when she looked at the empty store.

Doug stood right by her side as she negotiated the terms of the lease, and even provided some of his own finances toward the future of the store. She'd only been in town for one day, and she'd already managed to get an apartment and a future store. She had never experienced this kind of success before, and it made her thirsty for more, and more grateful than she could imagine. Tears of happiness came to her eyes as she felt her dreams coming true. It was a tin-gling that ran all the way through her ribcage, like she was being lifted up by her ribs and floating through the air.

Not all of her dreams became fulfilled in that moment, though. It was months before Virgil returned the divorce pa-pers, signed and notarized, and then it was finally over. Doug had to agree to child support, but his work as a contractor left him with enough money to support his children without falling into poverty. Eventually, she had a wonderful apart-ment, a new life, a husband that would protect her instead of hurting her, and she felt like her every need was fulfilled, but she didn't mind that things took time. It just made the re-wards of her new future that much more precious.

Doug got to work on the store right away. He was able to contract help to paint the walls in beautiful murals. He found people to make custom shelves that wouldn't get in the way. He even designed a playroom for the smaller children to just have fun while their parents were looking for books.

The nursery was the most important part of the store to Kelly. Even while she was handling customers, she could lis-ten to the little ones laughing, and the sound filled her heart with joy.

Even though the customers kept her busy, and more of

them began to arrive every week, she had to make all that a second priority when she felt a little baby kick the inside of her belly. She put her hand over her belly.

Now that was a real kick, and I'm actually going to have a baby.

The new life growing inside of her had avoided detection until that kick, but the moment she felt it, she got distracted. She was relieved to see that no one wanted her attention at the moment, but she was also sad that Doug was so busy at his new building contract to witness the moment. She wanted to tell him about it right away, but no customers interrupted her moment of awakening.

This one moment of awareness happened in total isolation, even though a customer walked through the door a few seconds later. In those moments of bliss, Kelly was completely alone with her new child.

When her baby was born, Kelly named the little girl Cheyenne, and when she was holding the girl in her arms for the first time, the little infant giggled and her little laugh was sweeter than all the laughing children she'd listened to in her store.

Only then did Kelly feel like her life was complete and that all her dreams had come true. The same thrill swept through her lungs just like the day she leased the store, and she knew that she had been waiting her entire life for this kind of happiness. She couldn't think of anything else that would make her life more amazing.

About the Author

Melissa Saari

Melissa Saari lives in Washington State where the Columbia River, the river that powers America, rushes near her front door, and every summer, smoke from forest fires fill the sky. These powerful elements inspire her writing, whether it's romance, fantasy, or horror.

Melissa also has two loving, protective dogs: a female pit bull named Marla and a male Chow called Leo. Her dogs provide comedy, therapy, and inspiration for her stories.

Melissa will always be a writer. She begins her Master's Degree in Screenwriting this fall to study the complex film industry and how her vision can be shared with billions of moviegoers.